**"Come away with me, my little petunia,"
Tom whispered comically as he pulled her
toward the orchard.**

"Tom, you crazy man," Helen said, laughing. "I can't just leave. I'm the hostess of this garden party."

"And are therefore entitled to certain privileges," he said.

"But I can't just—" she began firmly.

He brought her sharply against his chest with a determined yank, then leaned down to press his lips against hers. The kiss was brief and hard and incredibly sensual.

"Five minutes, Helen," he said against her lips, his voice husky. Then suddenly they were running. When they reached the orchard, he pulled her abruptly to a halt. Helen leaned against a tree, breathless from laughter and excitement. Suddenly Tom handed her an overflowing glass of champagne and gave her a devastating smile.

"I have a feeling you're a born troublemaker," she said with mock regret as she sipped the champagne.

Tom studied her for a moment, then tilted her head and bent to kiss drops of champagne from her lips. "That depends on what you call trouble . . ."

Bantam Books by Billie Green
Ask your bookseller for the titles you have missed.

A TRYST WITH MR. LINCOLN?
 (*Loveswept #7*)

A VERY RELUCTANT KNIGHT
 (*Loveswept #16*)

ONCE IN A BLUE MOON
 (*Loveswept #26*)

TEMPORARY ANGEL
 (*Loveswept #38*)

TO SEE THE DAISIES . . . FIRST
 (*Loveswept #43*)

THE LAST HERO
 (*Loveswept #65*)

THE COUNT FROM WISCONSIN
 (*Loveswept #75*)

DREAMS OF JOE
 (*Loveswept #87*)

A TOUGH ACT TO FOLLOW
 (*Loveswept #108*)

WHAT ARE *LOVESWEPT* ROMANCES?

They are stories of true romance and touching emotion. We believe those two very important ingredients are constants in our highly sensual and very believable stories in the *LOVESWEPT* line. Our goal is to give you, the reader, stories of consistently high quality that may sometimes make you laugh, sometimes make you cry, but are always fresh and creative and contain many delightful surprises within their pages.

Most romance fans read an enormous number of books. Those they truly love, they keep. Others may be traded with friends and soon forgotten. We hope that each *LOVESWEPT* romance will be a treasure—a "keeper." We will always try to publish

LOVE STORIES YOU'LL NEVER FORGET
BY AUTHORS YOU'LL ALWAYS REMEMBER

The Editors

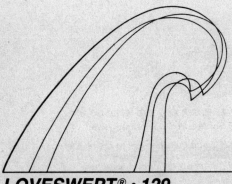

LOVESWEPT® • 129
Billie Green
Mrs. Gallagher and the Ne'er-do-well

BANTAM BOOKS
TORONTO • NEW YORK • LONDON • SYDNEY • AUCKLAND

MRS. GALLAGHER AND THE NE'ER-DO-WELL
A Bantam Book / February 1986

LOVESWEPT® and the wave device are registered
trademarks of Bantam Books, Inc. Registered in U.S. Patent
and Trademark Office and elsewhere.

All rights reserved.
Copyright © 1986 by Billie Green.
This book may not be reproduced in whole or in part, by
mimeograph or any other means, without permission.
For information address: Bantam Books, Inc.

ISBN 0-553-21743-7

Published simultaneously in the United States and Canada

Bantam Books are published by Bantam Books, Inc. Its
trademark, consisting of the words "Bantam Books" and
the portrayal of a rooster, is Registered in U.S. Patent and
Trademark Office and in other countries. Marca Registrada.
Bantam Books, Inc., 666 Fifth Avenue, New York, New
York 10103.

PRINTED IN THE UNITED STATES OF AMERICA

O   0 9 8 7 6 5 4 3 2 1

One

". . . and of course, the touch of green on this one will bring out the color of your eyes."

Helen glanced up at the two hats the saleswoman was holding up for her inspection. She considered pointing out that her eyes were pale blue without the slightest hint of green, but quickly discarded the idea. It simply wasn't worth the effort.

"Ann," Helen said, her voice thoughtful. "Isn't the black one exactly like the hat I bought last month?"

"Oh, no, Mrs. Gallagher." The saleswoman's eyes widened indignantly as though the very idea were outrageous. "That one had a red band."

"But . . ." Helen began, then again decided it wasn't worth the effort. "Yes, of course, it did."

Helen settled the sedate black hat over her smooth, blond hair, then leaned back to view it and her face below it. Familiarity caused her to skim over the even features without really taking them in. She knew her skin was smooth and clear, knew that not a hair of her golden blond chignon was out of place. Her makeup was the correct makeup for a respectable widow, her hairstyle the correct style. And the slim navy dress she was wearing was exactly what was right and proper for a woman of her standing in the community.

It was the look in her eyes that she was now examining. There was something there that she didn't understand. Something odd. Cynicism? Whatever it was, she had noticed it before, and it worried her. There was nothing in her life that warranted that expression.

A slight frown was beginning to form when she brought her thoughts back to the choice before her. Then to her astonishment she found that she was not alone in the mirror. There was another pair of eyes there. They were not blue, feminine, proper eyes but supremely masculine eyes that were dark brown, fringed with black. Eyes that were brimming over with fun.

For a moment she was too startled to move, too surprised to glance away from the bold eye contact. Her stare was wide-eyed, her face almost childlike in its openness as she took in the figure standing outside the shop, gazing at her through the plate-glass window.

He was a large man and, even dressed in worn jeans and a faded black T-shirt, he looked like a man in control. His hair was thick and a little too long at the back. The silver didn't take the form of distinguished streaks at the temples, but was salted throughout, adding sharp contrast to the black. His was not a handsome face, but it was compellingly rugged, attractive.

Suddenly, audaciously, he winked. Catching herself up sharply, Helen glanced away, pretending the moment hadn't happened. She purposely kept her gaze away from him, wondering how long he had been standing outside the store watching her. For he was very definitely watching her.

He wasn't from Langston; she was sure of it. This was not a man she would have overlooked in the town she knew so well. Something about him seemed foreign to East Texas. He was different, but Helen couldn't really put her finger on the reason she found him different. It could have been his clothes. Or perhaps it was simply the confident, casual way he held himself, as though the rest of the world could go to hell; and it wouldn't bother him one bit.

But still, there was nothing about him to cause alarm. So why was her heart beating so fast? For a woman as self-assured as Helen it was not a comfortable feeling, and she pulled herself up straighter, visibly stiffening her spine to combat the moment of unease.

She studied the hat, trying to keep her mind on the choice she should be making. Then irresistibly her gaze returned to the corner of the mirror. He was still there, still watching her. As their eyes met in the mirror his lips spread in a stunningly attractive smile.

Frowning, she averted her eyes and again tried to focus her attention on the hat. The man was simply bad-mannered, and she wouldn't let a stranger's rude behavior get to her. She was above that sort of thing, she told herself. Yes, she thought firmly, she would simply ignore him and he would go away.

But almost instantly her gaze returned to the man in the mirror. She watched from beneath her lashes as he leaned his head to the side, staring openly. Incredibly it looked as if he were considering the hat. Then, as though he knew he was holding her attention, he shook his head slowly from side to side in a gentle negative motion.

Her forehead creased in bewilderment; all pretense of ignoring him was now gone. She glanced at the hat, then raised a single questioning brow. Again, more emphatically, he shook his head, registering his disapproval.

Hesitantly she removed the rejected hat and picked up the second one Ann had brought. After holding up the plain gray suede—so that she could get a better look at it, *not* for his inspection—she placed it on her head. She stared at it for a moment, then leaned back to glance surreptitiously at her unexpected critic. He turned his head this way and that, considering the hat, then firmly shook his head. He looked as though he had just bitten into a sour pickle, and his expressive features almost made her laugh out loud. The hat definitely wouldn't do.

"Ann," Helen called out to the young woman, who had gone to the back of the shop. "These aren't right. Could you bring something . . . something different?"

Two minutes later Helen had a small mountain of hats beside her. Each was tried on with great deliberation, and each was rejected by her staunch critic as unworthy. He showed no signs of tiring of the game, and for reasons she wouldn't examine neither did she.

"No, Ann. These simply won't do," Helen said as she laid the last hat on the table. "I need a special hat." She swung around in her chair to gaze up at the puzzled woman. "A special hat," she repeated earnestly.

"Well, there is one . . ." Ann said, her face showing her doubt. "But I really don't think it's right for you."

"Let me see it."

"But—"

"I want to see it, Ann," she said firmly.

The saleswoman sighed with resignation. "Yes, Mrs. Gallagher. Whatever you say."

When she saw the hat, Helen's face was every bit as doubtful as Ann's. It was the brightest shade of teal blue she had ever seen. The brim was enormous, the rounded crown closely covered with small, iridescent feathers, and there was the tiniest, flirtiest bit of black veil, merely a scrap of seductive mesh to cover eyes that were suddenly the same shade of blue. It was a hat for a romantic interlude, a hat for a secret rendezvous.

After settling the outrageous article on her head, Helen slowly raised her eyes to the mirror, her head already beginning to move in a hesitant negative motion. But his enthusiastic nod of approval canceled her skepticism. When he lifted his hand, his thumb and forefinger were held together in an emphatic *okay* sign.

Before she realized what she was doing, Helen had bought the hat. The scandalous, flirtatious hat that was totally out of character for her.

As she walked to the door of the shop, her arm through the cord of the hatbox, she stopped abruptly. What on earth was she thinking of? Instead of freezing him with what her daughter called her "drop dead" look, Helen had actually encouraged a stranger's interest. What if he was still out there, waiting for her? What would she do then?

Drawing in a deep breath, Helen arranged her face in forbidding lines, opened the door, and walked out of the shop. The sidewalk was empty.

He wasn't anywhere in sight. Relief surged through her, then she pulled herself up short. Why was her heart pounding in such a peculiar manner? Why was she almost terrified at the thought of having to speak to a strange man? Had her life become so narrow that anything new threw her into a spin?

As she walked slowly away from the store she saw the familiar street, the familiar people, without really taking any of it in. She had bought a hat that was totally wrong for her. It would only sit in the closet and gather dust. Even more incomprehensible, she had had a wordless yet intimate—yes, she admitted, it had been intimate—conversation with a total stranger.

She shook her head. What had come over her? Oh, please, she begged silently. It couldn't be that awful stage that several of her friends had gone through. Widows like herself or divorcees, they had suddenly decided everyone but them was enjoying life and had frantically begun trying to recapture their youth. They had only succeeded in making fools of themselves.

Helen shuddered. She didn't want that to happen to her. Her friend Charlotte was going through it right now, and it hurt to see the amused looks that passed behind the woman's back. Not that she could really blame the people who made fun, Helen thought. Charlotte was flirting with every man in sight. The plump redhead dressed and acted like a teenager with hyperactive hormones. She had always been a little scatterbrained, but she had never before been an embarrassment to family and friends. Helen smiled sadly.

She would die if she were to become such an object of ridicule in this town, where people had always looked up to her. Her husband had been its mayor and leading citizen until his death five years earlier. He had been a good man, a respected man, and Helen had done everything in her power to carry on in his image. Now the town looked up to her in the same way.

Suddenly Helen caught sight of a tall, thin woman across the street and raised her hand in greeting, while at the same time squelching a frown. Althea Phillips was the self-appointed leader of the group who openly ridiculed Charlotte. Helen had never really liked Althea, but since she was president of the woman's club to which both Helen and Charlotte belonged, frequent contact with her was unavoidable, especially now when the club was beginning rehearsals for its annual musical.

"Good morning, Mrs. Gallagher," a child called.

Helen smiled at the passing children. "Good morning, Darryl, Pat." She loved kids, and because she loved them, it sometimes bothered her that they always spoke to her in reverent tones, as though she were a holy relic or something. They never let their natural exuberance show until they were out of her presence.

Her own children had shown no such restraint, she thought with a rueful smile. It was hard to believe that Audrey was a married woman now—married and with a child on the way. And Gary, her sweet lovable Gary, was in his second year at college. He was going to be a single-minded businessman just as his father had been. In a few years he would marry and start a family of his own. Logically Helen knew this would simply mean the enlargement of the family circle, but emotionally it felt as though she would be losing Gary. And Helen would have even more time to fill.

Oh, great, Helen thought wryly. She was beginning to sound sorry for herself, which was ridiculous. She had a good life. Oh, maybe sometimes she wished for the freedom to scratch her nose in public, and maybe sometimes her circle of friends seemed a little restricted. But she had lived in this small world for a long time, and she had no real wish to change it.

Oh, no? came the silent, unwanted question. *What about the nights?*

Helen shook off the thought. She didn't want to think about how lately, in the early hours of the morning while the rest of the world slept, she would awake with the crazy idea that a scream was forming inside her. It was an unpleasant sensation—an almost frightening sensation, because she couldn't find the reason for it.

Maybe I should consider taking a job, she thought. Years ago she had wanted to teach. Surely she could find something that would take her mind off the emptiness of her huge house, the house that Edward had given her, the house he had been so proud of. Even with Patty and Arnold, the couple who ran her home so beautifully, the house had a deserted feel to it. It smelled empty, like a faded chocolate box in an attic trunk.

"Honest, Officer, I have an explanation for this."

Helen's confident stride faltered when she heard the voice. It could have been because she knew everyone in town and knew this voice belonged to none of her fellow citizens, or it could have been something beyond her understanding. Whatever the reason, she knew the voice. Even before she glanced up, Helen knew it was the man in the mirror.

He was only a few steps away from her, standing beside a large white and green motor home as he talked to one of Langston's police officers. "There are extenuating circumstances. I was"—he broke off when he saw Helen approaching and smiled; a slow, sensual curving of strong lips—"I was waiting for a lady," he continued softly. "You can't fault me just because she's late." He leaned closer to the officer. "You know how women are."

When the policeman nodded in sympathy, Helen's eyes widened indignantly. The uniformed man turned, and when he saw her the humor in his eyes changed to alert respect. He hastily removed his hat. "I'm sorry, Mrs. Gallagher. I didn't know he was waiting for you."

"That's all right, Brad," she said softly.

When the young officer tipped his hat and left, Helen turned to the audacious stranger. The amused look in his dark eyes told her he harbored no misconceptions. He knew she was angry.

"Mrs. Gallagher," he said softly. "Now I wonder what goes with that. Deirdre? Paula? No, they're wrong. Something more regal." He studied her. "Helen. Yes, it's Helen. That face could definitely launch a thousand ships."

Her eyes narrowed suspiciously. "How did you know?"

"Your initials are on your purse. H.G." He nodded toward her leather bag. "Henrietta and Harriet are wrong. It had to be Helen."

The smile that softened her face took her by surprise. "Why couldn't it be Holly or Hepzibah?"

"Because I didn't think of them." His voice was guileless, but his eyes were sparkling with humor. "Besides, I know so much about you that your name comes easily."

She gave him a startled look. "What could you possibly know about me?"

"I know that you're a widow rather than a divorcee." He raised his chin and looked down his nose at her as though mocking her "regal" posture. "You couldn't possibly enter into anything so distasteful as divorce."

Helen made no comment. As it was, this man was too sure of himself; she wouldn't bolster his ego by confirming his wild guesses.

"And," he continued, "I know that your husband was someone important in this town." He laughed as she raised one arched brow in inquiry. "That one was easy. The policeman's reaction to you gave it away."

"Are you through?"

"No. I also know that you spend your time doing works of charity and"—he paused to consider her for a moment—"and playing bridge."

"I never play bridge," she said, her tone subdued. Then she realized she had merely succeeded in confirming his other assumptions. Before he could continue with his little game, she added, "Why did you lie to Brad, Mr. . . . ?"

"It's Tom Peters." He bowed, and although the gesture should have looked slightly ridiculous, it didn't. "Tom to you," he added softly.

"Why did you lie, Mr. Peters?"

"I wasn't lying. I was waiting for you. I've been waiting for you forever." The words were spoken simply, softly, sincerely, but a smile lurked on his lips, belying his tone.

She tilted her head to the right to view him curiously. "You're being very silly."

He shook his head. "I'm not being silly. I'm flirting."

Was that what he was doing? Helen was taken

aback. Had it been so long since anyone had flirted with her that she didn't recognize it? How was she supposed to act? Should she be outraged? She didn't feel outraged. But she had been thrown off-balance, and she didn't like it.

"You seem shocked by the idea," he said, his eyes laughing at her, even mocking her. "If the idea of flirting shocks you so much, why were you flirting with me when you were in the hat shop?"

She gasped. "I wasn't—"

"But you were," he corrected. "That's how I knew you weren't married. You wouldn't have flirted with me if you were married."

"I wasn't flirting," she said indignantly. "No . . ." She paused, her eyes widening. "Was I?"

"You were."

She was momentarily pleased that she could still do it and leaned forward to question him. Then, from the corner of her eye, she noticed people, across the street and in the shops, watching. Watching her. Closing her eyes briefly in embarrassment, she turned and began to walk away.

She was alone only for a moment. Then she sensed his presence and knew he was following her. The thickheaded idiot, she fumed silently. Couldn't he see that she was cutting him dead? She walked straight ahead, frantically trying to pretend he wasn't there.

"You look cute when you're indignant," he said suddenly. "Did you know that your nostrils twitch when you're trying to keep from saying something rude?"

Helen ignored the question. This was not a man

one took seriously. When she remained silent, she could feel his eyes on her. Then he began to speak in a soft voice, mimicking her Texas accent.

"Why, yes, Tom," he said. "I knew that. It's an inherited trait. My grandmother on my father's side was the nostril-twitching champion of Titus County."

Her lips quivered. She couldn't help it. He was funny. But she wouldn't give him the satisfaction of knowing she thought so. He wouldn't be slow to take advantage of it.

"You don't say," he continued in his own voice. "I've always envied people with talent."

Then his voice changed again, softening in imitation. "But, Tom, surely your incredible good looks and irresistible charm are talent enough?"

The laughter couldn't be held back now. However, when Helen saw Winifred Johnson, loan officer of the First National Bank, staring at her in astonishment, the laugh turned into a choking cough.

"Go away," she whispered urgently.

"Why?" The word was not said belligerently, but with genuine curiosity.

She turned to him. "People are watching us."

He glanced around. "So they are. Is that important?"

The question stopped her. She stood still and stared up at him. Was it important? she wondered suddenly, then shook her head in confusion.

"Yes. Yes, of course, it is." She was answering herself as well as him. "Good-bye, Mr. Peters."

She could feel him watching her as she walked away. When he spoke, she heard his words clearly and shivered.

"Later, Mrs. G."

Two

Tom was standing in the door of the Winnebago, a cup of coffee in one hand as he looked out on the wooded area surrounding his camping space. He liked East Texas. He liked the raucous sound of the bluejays and the extensive repertoire of the mockingbirds. He liked the clean smell of pine and the earthy smell of decaying vegetation. Maybe he would stay awhile.

Reaching behind him, he picked up the thin local paper and carried it to a picnic table. If he was going to stay, he would need a job.

The want ads barely covered a half page, but Tom wasn't worried. He always managed to find work. His needs were few. Minimum wage for hard physical labor would do just fine. Just so he had enough for food and gas.

Five minutes later two ads—the only temporary positions available—were circled in blue ink. Dishwasher or gardener, which would he be this time?

He had acted as both in the past. Washing dishes meant he would get his meals free. Gardening meant he would work in the open air, which was more appealing. He enjoyed any job that allowed him to stay outdoors.

He smiled, remembering the places he had seen, the people he had known. Especially the people. The majority had been good people, interesting people. People who had become the family he didn't have, the children and grandchildren he would never have.

He stood up and stretched, the hard muscles showing beneath his worn, gray sweatshirt and faded jeans. It was time for him to get moving. Although Tom always kept money aside for the hard times, he needed to find work to keep from dipping into that emergency fund.

He walked to the motorcycle that stood beside the special rack built on the rear of the Winnebago. He shrugged into the leather jacket draped over the handlebars, then pulled on the helmet.

As he rode along the winding asphalt roads of the small state park, he felt the way he had felt dozens of times before, in different climates, different surroundings. He felt as though nature—and life— were reaching out to enfold him. No, that was wrong. It wasn't anything as protective as enfolding; it was more like life was including him. He experienced a feeling of vitality he had never known before and found difficult to describe.

Once, early in his quest, he had felt the need to share the wonder of it all and had called one of his old friends. But almost immediately he knew something had changed. Although he and Hal were using the same language, Tom could no longer grasp what motivated his friend, and it was clear the opposite was also true. It was the last time he had tried to bridge the gap between the world he had left behind and the one he was living in now.

He smiled wryly as he neared the exit from the park. He couldn't imagine Hal applying for a job as a dishwasher.

Just outside the park stood a small grocery and tackle store with a gas pump out front. Adjoining it was a Laundromat, its turquoise-painted front peeling in large pieces. Tom pulled into the gravel parking lot in front of the Laundromat, close to the telephone booth attached to the outside wall.

Leaving his helmet behind, he carried the newspaper with him. Both ads gave only phone numbers. The advertisement for the gardening job instructed the applicant to call between eight and nine A.M. or after seven in the evening. The other ad held no restrictions, and because it offered the less desirable of the two jobs, he tried it first.

The position was still open. It was at a small café not far from the park. It would be convenient, but after a minute's conversation with the manager Tom knew that he did not want to work with the man. He had worked for some pretty hard taskmasters—men who required one hundred and fifty percent from their employees, and Tom had gotten along with them just fine. But this man was slovenly even in conversation.

Tom wasn't about to close any doors, but his fingers were crossed as he dialed the second number.

"Yeah."

The word was shouted at such a volume that Tom almost dropped the phone. He grinned and said, "You advertised for a gardener's helper. Is the job still open?"

"Yeah."

This time he was ready for the response and wasn't startled by the loudness. The voice was that of an older man, and Tom guessed he was either hard of hearing or used to talking to people who were. Or maybe he just didn't trust telephones.

"I'd like to apply," Tom said, carefully keeping the laughter out of his voice.

"Fine by me," the old man said. "Doesn't mean I'll give you the job. What's your name?"

"Tom. Tom Peters."

"I'm Joe, just plain Joe. Never been called anything else. No need to start now." He paused and Tom could almost see his eyes narrowing in suspicion. "You're not from around here. I knew it from your voice and your name shows I'm right. No Tom Petry around here."

"It's Peters, Mr.—Joe. Not Petry."

"Doesn't make any difference," Joe said gruffly. "I'll warn you right now, it's a temporary job and I'm a mite particular about who works for me."

"Fine by me," Tom said, chuckling openly. "When can I come out to talk to you?"

"You got any plans for the next thirty minutes?" the old man asked dryly.

A man of action, Tom thought. This was a man he would enjoy working with. "Not a one. How do I get there?"

He fumbled in his pocket for a pen as the old man began to shout directions rapidly. Tom had barely written down the address when Joe indicated he had other, more important things to do.

"Pull around behind the house," Joe shouted. "You won't have any trouble finding me; I'll be the one that's earning my keep." He grumbled something about freeloaders and hung up.

The residential district to which Joe had directed Tom was set among rolling, wooded hills. The homes were large and stately with precisely manicured lawns and lots of ivy. It reminded him of the area of Upstate New York where he had lived until a year ago. The foliage might be different, but the atmosphere was the same. Old names, old money.

The occupant of a slow-moving patrol car eyed him carefully as he passed. Apparently the wealthy were well guarded in this town, he thought in amusement. Tom turned onto Pinetree Avenue and began glancing at the numbers on the passing mailboxes. He was looking for 1001.

He almost missed it. The mailbox was set in a rock wall that surrounded the estate, and the numbers were almost covered by trailing ivy. Pulling over to the side, he put down the kickstand and walked to the mailbox. The brass plate above the mailbox read MR. AND MRS. EDWARD GALLAGHER.

Tom smiled slowly. Could it be the same Gallagher, Helen of the blue eyes, who wanted so badly to laugh but didn't know how to free herself to do so? He had known he would see her again, but he'd expected to have to hunt for her. This was better, he decided. Now he knew he would get the job. Fate was taking a hand, he thought, and in this instance fate and Tom were in perfect agreement.

The old man had told him to drive to the back entrance, but he hadn't told him that the "backyard" was a minipark. The cement drive widened at the end to form a small parking lot to one side of the four-car garage. A variety of trucks and cars was parked there, evidently driven by day help and delivery people.

Tom left his motorcycle next to an electrical supply truck and looked toward the house, which had not been visible from the street. It was a three-story English Tudor on a grand scale. Extending to the back of the house on the right side was a solarium, its glass walls shining brightly in the morning sun. On the left the house was covered with heavy flowering vines that climbed to a wide second-story balcony.

The right side of the grounds seemed to be the practical side. A vegetable garden and a greenhouse were in the foreground, and beyond that Tom could see fruit trees. To the left were the formal gardens, where flowers and shrubs were perfectly manicured to show what nature could do when man took a hand in cultivating it.

Tom started up the stone walk toward the house, then noticed a man bent over an azalea bush and moved toward him. The old man wore faded overalls; a stained felt hat covered his head, and tufts of white hair stuck out here and there beneath the narrow brim.

MRS. GALLAGHER AND THE NE'ER-DO-WELL

Tom cleared his throat and the old man looked up.

"You Peters?" he boomed.

Tom nodded, grinning as Joe began to examine him.

"Well, you look strong enough for the work." His eyes narrowed suspiciously as he stared at Tom's face. "Why do you want this job?"

"So I can eat," Tom said, his grin widening.

"Good a reason as any, I guess," the old man said gruffly. "It's only temporary. It's my nephew Howie's job, but he's laid up for a few weeks."

"Yes, you made that clear when we talked earlier. I only need a temporary job."

"Well, by the looks of you"—the old man's eyes passed over him, gauging his size and strength—"you could handle it. You don't need a lot of brains for the job. Just a strong back. That's what my nephew's got: no brains but a strong back." He looked at Tom again, his lined face looking incredibly shrewd. "You talk like an educated man. How come you want a job like this? Why not a fancy desk job?"

"I like working outdoors. I like the smell of dirt and watching things grow." He shrugged. "And as I said, I like to eat."

There was understanding in the old man's eyes. Apparently he loved growing things too. "Okay, you got the job. Where you stayin'?"

Tom nodded to the east. "I've got a motor home parked over at the state park."

"I'll talk to Mrs. Gallagher about lettin' you park it back there." He waved toward the cement drive.

"To tell you the truth some days we work clear till dark. Being here would save you some time and money."

"I'd appreciate that." Tom hesitated. He almost asked if this Mrs. Gallagher and his Mrs. Gallagher were the same, but he let it go. He could wait. Instead, he brought up the question of his salary, and when that was settled, he asked, "Do you take care of this whole place by yourself?"

"Nah," he said, giving a snort that could have been amusement or disdain. "Frank and his boys work the vegetable garden and the fruit trees. I take care of the rest. When I need help, an unexpected frost or something, some of the high school boys come out. It doesn't happen too often, thank the good Lord. I like to take care of my plants by myself. I know 'em, know what they like and what they don't like."

The old man's gaze had wandered to the azalea bush and then, as though Tom had been forgotten, Joe suddenly turned back to his work.

"When do you want me to start?"

The gardener looked over his shoulder with obvious reluctance. "You got any objection to right now? I could use a hand with some fertilizer."

Tom stripped off his jacket and threw it on a wrought-iron chair. "Right now's fine."

"Helen, are you listening?"

Helen blinked as though coming awake, then glanced at her secretary. She hadn't been listening. She had been caught up in the view from the study window. Spring had come so suddenly this year. There were colors and fragrances today that had been absent yesterday.

She smiled and shook her head. "I'm sorry, Terri. I think I've got a full-blown case of spring fever. What were you saying?"

The petite woman gave her a sympathetic smile. "I asked if you wanted me to talk to Joseph about flowers for the party. The roses will be just right, but he needs to know which ones you want. You know how testy he gets when we don't give him enough notice."

Helen smiled as she thought of the gruff old man who had been with her for twenty years. "No, I'll speak to him. I want to look around the garden and the greenhouse. Maybe I'll come up with some new ideas. I can't seem to work up the proper enthusiasm."

"But you love parties!"

She nodded. "I always have. But when I think of this one, it seems like a rerun of all the others. . . ." Her voice trailed away softly; then she noticed the look of concern in Terri's eyes. "Don't worry. Like I said, it's just spring fever."

"Well, I don't know why you should be immune. It's something that affects everyone." She grinned. "To tell you the truth I keep having thoughts of picnics and long hikes in the woods myself."

Helen stood. "Maybe a walk through the gardens will get me back on the right track."

She moved to the French doors that opened onto the terrace and stepped through. Outside the sounds of spring were as vibrant as the colors. She walked toward the work noises to her right.

"Joe—"

Helen stopped abruptly, inhaling sharply when she saw the man bending over her flower bed. It wasn't Joe. It wasn't anyone who should be there. It was the outrageous man from the hat store. The man who had followed her the day before. And he was elbow deep in dirt—*her* dirt.

"What on earth are you doing here?"

His head swiveled to glance up at her, then he leaned back on his heels. "Working."

"I can see that." Her voice was exasperated. "But why? How?"

He shrugged. The movement was casual, but his eyes never left her face. "Your gardener advertised for a helper. I took the job."

"You're a gardener?"

"And a plumber and a truck driver and a road builder." His eyes moved over her, then he smiled. It was an outrageously sensual smile. "I guess I could be just about anything you want." He studied her face for a moment. "You look surprised. What did you think I was?"

The question left her confused. Brushing a strand of hair from her eyes, she said, "I don't know." She shook her head. "I don't think I thought about it at all. But I would never have guessed you were a . . ."

"A drifter?" he offered when she hesitated. "A vagabond? A ne'er-do-well?"

"Is that what you are?"

"You could say so. In fact, you probably would

say so. I stay in one place for as long as I want, then I move on." He smiled as though he knew something she didn't. "I call it freedom, but then I suppose a thing looks different depending on the vantage point you're viewing it from."

As they talked his eyes kept wandering over her, several times lingering on the white jump suit she wore, as though in some way it displeased him. She frowned. She was his employer, for heaven's sake. But suddenly she didn't feel like his employer; she merely felt like a woman. It was something in his expression as he stared at her.

Part of her resented the intimacy of that stare; but another part—a part she hadn't known still survived—was undeniably exhilarated. This was the part she tried to squelch, but she couldn't find the strength to look away from those dark, knowing eyes.

By staying, by not removing herself from the situation, she tacitly gave him permission to continue. His visual exploration of her body became more blatant. It seemed as though he had discarded the white jump suit and had begun to examine the woman beneath, the flesh and blood and bones that went together to make Helen Gallagher.

Not once during his exploration did she feel that he was insulting her. It was not that kind of thing at all. She felt the heat of his gaze on her breasts, on her thighs, but her overriding emotion was curiosity. What did he think of her? What did he think of the woman within that he was examining so carefully?

The security of her standing in the community,

the security of old, trusted friends, wasn't present now. He was delving deeper, to the source of her individuality. Did he find her lacking? Was she a copy of all her friends?

As though he sensed her sudden insecurity, his stare became caressing, stroking her, soothing her. Incredibly she was as responsive to the look in his eyes as a puppet to a puppetmaster. Then, with a lightning switch of moods that left her breathless, desire emanated from him, touching something in her she had thought untouchable, pulling at her, forcing her to share what he was feeling. A deep, burning ache spread through her. The sensation was so powerful, she actually took a step forward, answering an unspoken summons.

"Mother."

Helen's eyes widened in shock, and a shudder shook her when she realized what had almost happened. She turned in relief as her daughter's voice abruptly released her from the spell.

The young woman approaching them suddenly stopped walking, glancing first at Helen, then at Tom. "Patty said you were out here talking to Joe." She looked around pointedly.

"Audrey, this is Tom Peters." Helen avoided his eyes, wanting to wipe out what had gone before. But she knew he heard the unsteadiness in her voice. "He'll be helping Joe in the garden until Howie recuperates."

"Hello," Audrey said, her eyes frankly assessing.

"Hello, yourself," he said, smiling as though amused by her obvious interest. "If you'll excuse me, I need to get another sack of wood chips."

Audrey watched him walk away. "Mother," she whispered, "he's *gorgeous*."

Helen hid her smile and shook her head in parental disapproval. "I don't really think Chad would appreciate your noticing that."

"I'm married, not dead," the younger woman quipped. Her tone was flippant, but she sighed discontentedly at the mention of her husband's name. "Chad probably wouldn't even notice that I noticed."

"Come on," Helen said, sliding her arm around her daughter's burgeoning waist. "Let's have coffee and we can talk." They walked together through the study and into the spacious living room. "Sit down while I go tell Patty to bring some in."

Audrey grinned. "I've already told her. She said she would have to make a fresh batch."

Helen studied her daughter's delicate features. There were dark circles under her eyes and lines of dissatisfaction around her mouth. "Okay, Audrey, talk. What's wrong between you and Chad?"

"There's nothing wrong with Chad," she said sarcastically, her expression unattractive. "Didn't you know he's perfect? And as for me, perfect Chad tells me my hormones are out of whack because of the baby."

"Come on, Audrey. Tell me."

"That's it, Mother," she said, her voice exasperated. "It's just exactly as I've told you. When I try to talk about our problems, Chad says we have no problems—that I'm being overemotional." She moved restlessly on the couch. "Lord, if he says that one more time, I swear I'll show him what overemotional really looks like."

Helen smiled. Her daughter's temper was notorious. "Okay, so you can't talk to him about what's bothering you. Talk to me. You know Dr. Goode said you were to avoid stress. You need to get it out of your system or you take a chance of complicating your pregnancy."

She sighed. "Oh, Mother, everything's all wrong. One of the reasons I fell in love with Chad was his outlook on life. I was important to him. I was the most important thing to him. I never thought he would get so wrapped up in his work." She tightened her hands into fists. "I never thought he would turn out to be like Daddy."

Helen glanced up sharply. "Your father was a wonderful man who loved you and Gary very much. Why would you say a thing like that?"

Audrey sighed again, this time in frustration. "I'm sorry, Mother. I know you think that Daddy was perfect, but couldn't you see the way he neglected us, neglected you?"

"We were never neglected," Helen stated, slowly and firmly.

"Okay, maybe that was a little harsh," Audrey admitted. "But didn't you ever feel that we came last? First was his insurance company, then his role as mayor, then his friends at the country club, and *then* his family."

"You're wrong," Helen said softly. "Yes, he was ambitious, and yes, he devoted a lot of time to business, but we were always in his thoughts."

Audrey laughed, and the bitterness of the sound

shocked Helen. "That's what you always told us. When he missed my tenth birthday you said, 'He can't be here, but he's thinking of you.' When he missed every one of Gary's baseball games, you would always say, 'Something came up, but he's thinking of you.' Mother, we didn't want his thoughts, we wanted him. I always wanted to say 'Why can't he be with us and just think of work?' I would have liked that better."

"Okay, I get your point," Helen said, unwilling to argue about Edward. He was gone and changing Audrey's view of the past was not the point of this conversation. "Would you like me to talk to Chad?" Helen offered reluctantly.

Audrey moved to kneel beside her mother, her expression hopeful. "Oh, Mother, could you? He thinks you're terrific. He listens to you. If you tell him he's wrong, I just know he'll stop."

Helen shook her head. "I can't tell him he's wrong." When her daughter started to protest, she continued. "He's a man, Audrey. I refuse to treat him like a child. But I will find out why this is so important to him. Maybe that will help you deal with it."

Audrey laid her head in Helen's lap as she had done so many times in years past. "I wish I could be more like you," she whispered. "I try and I try, but I always fail." She raised her eyes to her mother. "You're so . . . so good."

"Audrey!" Helen said. "I'm no such thing. I don't want you to be like me. You're perfectly wonderful just as you are."

Helen was almost relieved when Patty chose that

moment to bring in the coffee. By the time the stocky housekeeper had left, they'd gone on to new topics, and Audrey's tension seemed to have dissipated.

Audrey's enthusiasm was attractive, Helen noted, but sometimes her emotional highs and lows caused anxiety for the people who loved her. However, this time it appeared there was a very real cause for her upset, Helen thought. She would find a chance to talk to Chad at the party.

"You two will be here next Friday, won't you?" Helen asked. "Chad won't be working late?"

"He'll work late over my dead body," Audrey said. When her mother frowned, she laughed. "Don't worry. He promised he would be home early. We wouldn't miss it." She paused, then with a sly look in her eyes, added, "It's a good thing Gary decided not to come home for your party."

"Oh?" She knew her daughter, and the expression on Audrey's face told Helen she was about to say something provocative.

"If he gets one look at the new gardener, he'll explode," she said, then giggled in a way that took Helen back to the past, when Audrey was a little girl.

She gave her daughter an indulgent look. "Since when has Gary taken such an avid interest in the garden?"

Audrey stared impatiently at her mother. "Not the garden—*you.* Tom looks at you like you're a woman. Gary thinks you're completely asexual, and that you exist only for his benefit."

Helen laughed nervously, unwilling to remember

the way she had felt in the garden. "Gary's going through another stage. He'll grow out of his possessiveness. Probably when he finds a girl to fall in love with."

"Maybe," Audrey said, shrugging, "but there could be fireworks if he sees the way Tom looks at you . . . and the way you look back at him."

Helen kept her expression neutral, but confusion was filling her mind. Everything seemed off-balance. She had always been in control of her life. That control was her security. Now suddenly everything was changing. She was plagued by the urge to tell everyone—her daughter, Althea Phillips, *the world*—to leave her alone. Her life was not supposed to be like this. And although she knew she was being unreasonable, she felt it had all started the minute she had seen a stranger's eyes in a mirror.

Three

Helen touched the yellow roses that filled the large vase in the hall. The house smelled of roses. She always had fresh flowers, but today they were everywhere.

The party the night before had been a great success. The food was exquisite, the wine perfect. It had been just exactly like a hundred other parties in years past, Helen mused; the same people, the same conversations.

She turned away, shrugging in exasperation at her thoughts. Even if the party had been slightly dull for her, nonetheless she valued the efforts of her staff. She had already expressed her appreciation to Patty and Arnold. Now she needed to tell Joe and Tom how much the flowers they had provided had helped to guarantee the success of the party.

Silently she admitted she was putting it off because of Tom. He had been working with Joe for a week. And for a week she had watched him from the shadows of her balcony. Almost every evening he sat outside his motor home, softly playing a worn guitar. Sometimes Patty and Arnold or one of the maids would join him, but the presence or absence of an audience seemed to make no difference in his performance.

She frowned. What was it about the man that drew people to him? She admitted he had a certain charm, but he was also an irresponsible drifter, a man to avoid. And so far Helen had managed to do just that.

Simply knowing he was on the premises was enough to disrupt the regular pattern of her life. At odd times she would find herself at a window, watching him. He seemed to have an aversion to clothes. During his first day on the job he had worn a T-shirt and jeans. Then the jeans had become worn cutoffs, the shirt sleeveless. Finally the shirt had been discarded entirely. Helen didn't know his age—it could have been anywhere from late thirties to early fifties—but it seemed indecent for a man of his years to look so unashamedly sexual.

Yes, he was definitely a man to avoid, she thought, frowning. But now she was carrying avoidance too far. Tom had worked just as hard as Joe to provide flowers from the greenhouse and to get the grounds ready for the party. He deserved her thanks.

Drawing in a deep breath, Helen walked through the French doors and out onto the terrace. She saw him immediately. He was stooped over, repairing the damage a careless guest had done to a bed of violets. Reluctantly she moved to stand directly behind him.

"Tom," she said, her features under strict control.

He glanced up. "Mrs. Gallagher," he replied. His face was equally expressionless, but she suspected that inwardly he was once again laughing at her.

She stared at a space over his head. "I want to thank you for the work you've done in the garden. My guests last night were very complimentary."

"Thank you, ma'am."

Something in his bland tone caused her to lower her gaze to his face. Helen knew she should simply walk away, but she found herself murmuring, more to herself than to him, "Why do I always get the feeling that I amuse you?"

He rocked back on his heels, his eyes running over her, lingering on her pink silk blouse and white linen slacks as though he found something lacking there.

"You don't amuse me," he corrected. "No, I wouldn't put it that way at all." He smiled openly now. "Let's say your sterility intrigues me."

"Sterility?" She didn't like the sound of the word. She felt she had been insulted.

"Do you know how often you wear white?" he continued as he stood up, softly slapping his hands together to remove the loose earth. "It's as though you're saying no dirt would have the nerve to land on your clothes." One corner of his mouth turned up in a rueful smile. "Your spotless white clothes match your spotless reputation."

"And you think that's wrong?"

"Not wrong. Intriguing." His eyes remained on her face as he shook his head in amazement. "Do you know that there are no lines on your face? You have two grown children, but you're still brand-new. There is no clue to your life in your face. I know it's none of my business—"

That was enough. She knew she shouldn't have stayed. The man was determined to make her uncomfortable. "You're right, it isn't," she said stiffly, turning to leave.

Without discernible movement he caught her arm, then continued as though she hadn't spoken. "—but it makes me sad to see such a waste."

His tone of voice was soft, and Helen felt she was viewing the scene in slow motion as he leaned closer. "Are you in there, Helen?" He ran his index finger down her cheek. "Are you in there hiding behind this perfect mask?"

"What are you doing?" she gasped in outrage. "How dare you touch me!" She jerked her arm out of his grasp. "And how dare you talk to me about hiding. What are you hiding from, Mr. Peters? You've got a lot of nerve criticizing me. You, a drifter. A—a nobody!"

Swiveling sharply, she rushed toward the house, but before she had taken three steps he was beside her. He grabbed her shoulders and jerked her around. Then he held her chin in one hand, forcing her to look up at him.

"You can't leave yet, Mrs. G." His voice was low, and for once the humor was absent. "I'm sure you don't allow yourself to come in contact with a nobody very often. Aren't you curious? Don't you want to know how a nobody feels? Wouldn't you like to find out how a nobody kisses?"

"No!" The word was cut off in her throat as he lowered his lips to hers. It was a shock, physically and mentally. No one of her acquaintance would have had the nerve to do such a thing. The unbelievability of the situation robbed her of protest.

Yes, it was a shock. But after the first few seconds it was not shock that held her still. It was the feel of his lips on hers. She had known the moment she saw him outside the hat shop window that he was audacious, but the audacity of his lips and tongue astounded her.

She should be fighting him, Helen told herself. She should be trying to tell him that this was not what she wanted. But suddenly she didn't know if that was the truth. As his firm lips moved on hers she wondered if this wasn't something she had been wanting for years, needing for years. Then all thought stopped, and she moved closer to him, welcoming his arms around her.

Tom felt the small movement and almost groaned. He had intended to shock her into opening her eyes to him, to the world. He wanted to surprise her out of that cool detachment that she habitually assumed. But the minute his lips touched hers, he forgot all about teaching lessons. Instead, he felt as though she were teaching him, teaching him that this warmth was another part of life, a part he had overlooked. With her lips, her arms, she was forcing him out into the open. He thought he was so free. But there was no freedom without sharing, touching, giving.

Helen was breathless when he finally moved his lips away from hers. And as much as she hated to admit it, she instantly missed the feel of his body. His mouth was only a fraction of an inch away when he whispered shakily, "You certainly pack a wallop . . . for such a proper lady."

She laughed, her eyes revealing the excitement that was surging through her veins.

"There," he said huskily, staring at her face in satisfaction. "Now you're making some really interesting wrinkles." He glanced down at her blouse. "You also have some nice smudges on your clothes."

She followed his gaze downward, and suddenly her face turned pink. The dirt on her blouse and slacks brought a vivid recollection of the way she had felt when he'd touched her. She was still staring at the smudges when Patty walked up to her.

"Mrs. Gallagher, Charlotte Black is calling. Do you want me to bring a phone out here?"

"No," she said, her voice sounding hoarse. "No, I'll take it in the study." Without looking at Tom, she turned and walked away.

His kiss, his words, stayed with Helen throughout the day. At bedtime she studied her face in the mirror as she brushed out her hair. The silken mass fell well below her shoulders and gave her a softer, more feminine look as did the creamy flesh of her shoulders above her nightgown. But she didn't want to look at the white satin gown she wore. *White*, she thought, frowning.

The light from the bedside lamp fell across her even features. Was it a dull face? she wondered suddenly. Helen had never thought of it before, but at forty-two surely she should have more lines. Charlotte was older than she, and her face showed it. She had deep grooves around her mouth and a scattering of fine lines around her eyes. But then Charlotte was always either laughing or crying. Helen didn't think she would like living on that kind of emotional roller coaster.

She laid the brush down sharply. She couldn't believe what she was doing. She was taking seriously the words of a gardener's helper, a nothing, a self-professed drifter.

"Oh, hell," she swore softly. She was doing it again. That afternoon she had sounded like the worst kind of snob. She had sounded like the kind of person she most detested. The fact that he had provoked her didn't make it any easier for her to accept her own rudeness.

But Helen didn't want to think of that afternoon. She could make excuses for her pompous behavior, but there were no excuses for the way she had acted when Tom kissed her: Her behavior had been unforgivably wanton.

She ran her hands through her hair, pulling at the strands, hoping the pain would clear her mind. Why couldn't she forget it, forget him? Her steps were jerky, reflecting her irritation, as she walked out onto the balcony.

Then gradually her steps slowed. Flowering vines climbed the trellis below and spilled over the balcony rail; moonlight picked up the white flowers and her white gown, turning them silver and making the balcony an enchanted place.

The atmosphere calmed her. Tom Peters had nothing to do with her, she decided, her shoulder muscles relaxing with the thought. In a few weeks he would be gone, and she would be comfortable again. Until then she would simply stay out of his way.

She stood looking out over the orderly grounds. The smell of spring was in the air. It was the smell of renewal. Perhaps that was why she was beginning to feel dissatisfied with her life. Perhaps it was time for a personal renewal.

A movement among the flowers caught her attention first. Then she heard the sound of rustling leaves. For a moment her heart stood still. Then a head appeared above the railing, framed by white flowers and green leaves.

"Tom," she gasped, "what on earth . . . ?"

"I was in the neighborhood and just thought I would drop by," he said, sounding out of breath.

"You'll kill yourself," she whispered urgently.

Leaning over, she grabbed one of his arms and began pulling at it. He fell more than climbed onto the balcony, taking her down with him. His weight robbed her of breath; and his unexpected intrusion into her privacy robbed her of coherent thought.

He raised himself up on one elbow, smiling as he stared down at her. "I brought you a flower to apologize for my rudeness earlier, but it fell out of my mouth during the climb."

Helen tried to frown. She tried very hard. But she couldn't. A reluctant, hesitant laugh escaped her. "You're crazy," she murmured. And to her chagrin the words sounded complimentary rather than disapproving as she had intended.

Suddenly there was a strange, soft look in his eyes. "Sometimes I think so. But not when you laugh." Reaching up, he touched her mouth gently with his thumb. "Why don't you laugh more often, Helen? It's not that you seem sad; that would be human. But you seem to have simply opted out. Of life. Of emotion."

Tom sensed her withdrawal even before it showed on her face. "Hell," he said ruefully, rolling away from her to stand up. He offered her his hand and pulled her to her feet. "I'm doing it again, aren't I?"

"Yes, you are." She avoided his eyes as she smoothed the fabric of her gown with a hand that was shaking slightly.

"Don't do that," he said sharply, catching her hand. "It's all right to be rumpled, Helen." At her indignant glance he exhaled harshly. "Well, you invite it. Haven't you ever looked out the window after a snowfall and felt an itch to run out and leave your footprints in the snow?"

"You want to leave footprints on me?"

He laughed. "That's not what I meant, but I'm glad to see you can joke." He leaned closer, his voice confidential as he said, "I was beginning to think you had no sense of humor."

"Oh, I definitely have one," she said, frowning as she glanced up at him. "It's the only thing that keeps me from firing you. Watching you is better than watching Laurel and Hardy."

"Are you insinuating that I'm a clown? I'll have

you know that beneath this rough exterior lies the heart of a poet. How can you laugh at a poet?"

"Do you really write poetry?"

"Sure," he said, then he grinned. "Actually it's pretty bad poetry. I write what pleases me, regardless of proper form."

"Somehow I would have known that even without your telling me," she said, smiling. "Give me an example."

He thought for a moment. "Okay. Since we were talking about snow, I'll recite a poem of my own composition entitled 'Snowfall.' "

He cleared his throat and stood up straighter, bringing back memories of high school English class.

" 'Snowfall' by Thomas Edwin Peters. 'Charcoal-drawn trees. Dilapidated houses looking suddenly picturesque. Fenceposts dressed for evening in white velvet hats.' " He turned his eyes toward Helen. " 'Crisp white sheets, waiting to be mussed by ardent lovers.' "

She sucked in a sharp breath. "I should have known," she muttered. "I was beginning to be impressed by your sensitivity; then you revert to type."

"Yes, you should have known. I said I was a poet, not a marble statue. It wouldn't hurt you to 'revert to type' a little more often." Suddenly a look of excitement grew in his eyes. "Do something crazy with me, Helen. Just this once, do something crazy."

She backed away warily. "What are you talking about?"

"I'm not suggesting that you help me knock off a bank or—or fly to Zanzibar, for heaven's sake," he said, his voice faintly exasperated. "But for once in your life couldn't you do something on the spur of the moment?"

"Like what?" She didn't trust the look in his eyes. It was a crazy look, a wild look.

"Come for a moonlight ride on my trusty steed."

"Steed? You don't have a hor—" She broke off, her eyes widening as she backed against the wall. "You mean, your motorcycle?"

He laughed at her astonishment. "No one will see you, sweet Helen. Everyone in the house is asleep. Even the birds are asleep. No one will know that for a few minutes you forgot to be the proper Widow Gallagher." He leaned closer, placing a hand on the wall beside her head, trapping her simply by the strength of his presence. When he continued, his voice was soft and persuasive. "There's a wildness in you tonight, too, Helen. No, don't deny it," he said as she began to protest. "It's in your eyes. Take a chance, Helen. Let me show you how it feels to be really free . . . just for a little while."

His nearness was maddening and provoked strange reactions in Helen. It made her blood sing and the hairs on the back of her neck stand up crazily. His dark eyes held hers, and she couldn't look away. She didn't *want* to look away. Right that minute, right that second, if he had asked her to fly with him to Zanzibar, she would have gone.

She felt his excitement filling her, moving her to madness. Looking deep into his eyes, she whispered, "Yes . . . yes, I'll go." Then she laughed, almost in relief. "Yes, I will."

Tom almost didn't catch the words, so steeled was he for her rejection. He felt her acceptance rip through him as a physical power, as though her answer were more—much, much more—than a simple agreement to go for a moonlight ride. He wanted to grab her and squeeze her until she couldn't breathe, but he was afraid of frightening her into changing her mind.

"That's wonderful." His voice sounded harsh, raspy, so he repeated the last word: "Wonderful."

Suddenly there were no more words, and he simply stared at her. With her hair falling loosely about her shoulders she looked more open, more vulnerable. He had avoided looking at her body, knowing the reaction it would provoke. But now he had no control over his actions. His gaze slid over the creamy flesh of her shoulders above the white satin, then dropped slowly to her breasts.

Total nudity might have been lovelier, but it couldn't have been more provocative. The smooth, rounded tops of her breasts showed in the deep **V** of her gown, blending with the white satin. Her nipples stood out distinctly, pressing against the satin, adding to the wildness in his blood.

What would she do if he leaned down and took one of those tight nipples in his mouth, if he teased it with his tongue through the softness of her gown? What would she feel at his touch? What would she say when she saw the damp spot his mouth had caused?

Tom closed his eyes tightly and forced sanity to

return. He cleared his throat as he reluctantly moved away from her.

Her laugh was nervous. "Are you . . . are you going to recite more poetry?"

If her laugh was nervous, his was almost frantic. "No," he said hoarsely, his voice rueful. "But I think I'd better go before I get into trouble again."

Before Helen could think of a reply, he turned and moved to the balcony railing. A shiver of reaction ran down her spine, and it was a second before she could think logically. "You're not going to climb down?" she asked in astonishment. "There's no need for that. I can let you out downstairs."

Straddling the rail, he glanced at her over his shoulder. "There is a need." He laughed softly when he thought of walking through her bedroom. "Oh, yes, there is very definitely a need. I need the distraction of physical activity, and I need it right now."

He lowered himself over the rail, then his eyes sought hers. "And Helen?"

"Yes?"

"I'm not a strong person. Wear something bulky—and ugly." With that his head disappeared from sight.

She stood for a moment watching the spot where he had been. Then she laughed and spun around, walking quickly to the bedroom. Giving herself no time for doubts, she ripped the gown over her head and threw it on the bed. She pulled a pair of white slacks from the closet, then stopped abruptly and returned them to their hanger. Not white, she thought. Not tonight.

She dressed quickly in black slacks and a black sweater, then pulled her hair into a neat twist at the back of her head. Turning, she laughed softly at her image in the mirror. She looked like a cat burglar, she thought. A fitting companion for a second-story man, she thought, grinning as she walked out of her bedroom.

The stealthy trip down the stairs added to the feeling of adventure. She was laughing breathlessly as she ran out the front door, wrapping a black scarf around her hair.

Tom stepped out of the darkness and caught her in his arms, swinging her around a corner to where the motorcycle was waiting. "You won't be needing this," he whispered, pulling the scarf from her head. "Or these." One by one he drew the hairpins out of her hair, then ran his fingers through the golden mass to free it from confinement.

Holding her by the shoulders, he stared down at her. "Better," he said. "Much better." He turned and drew her toward the bike. "Now it's time for adventure."

Like eagles soaring in the wind they flew down country lanes, speeding past shadowy pines and open, moonlit fields. The wonderful sensation of her hair whipping wildly around her face became a symbol of the freedom she felt on the late-night ride.

Time lost all meaning for them. They traveled beyond time, beyond convention. She pressed her face to his broad back and let him take her where he wished, putting everything but the moment from her mind.

The moon was much lower in the sky when Tom pulled off a dirt road that ran beside a small lake. When he reached down to switch off the ignition, the silence around them seemed absolute. Then gradually the night sounds began to make themselves heard.

A solitary frog began to croak. Then one by one, others joined in until their hoarse songs filled the night.

Taking Helen by the hand, Tom led her to a small grassy rise where their view of the lake was unhampered by the shrubbery that grew thickly on the bank. Neither spoke, because speaking would have halted the symphony of the frogs, but more because words would have been superfluous.

For a long time they simply sat, arms wrapped around their knees, and listened. Then they began to speak in lazy whispers, blending their voices with the voices of the night as Tom told her of his travels.

"So," she murmured drowsily, "what came after North Dakota?"

"South Dakota, of course."

Tom's head was in her lap. When he had first moved it there, Helen had been startled. But gradually she'd come to accept it as part of the incredible night.

"South Dakota was where I met Ephram," he continued.

"Honest?" she asked, laughing softly. "Surely no one would really name an infant Ephram."

"I don't think Ephram was ever an infant. I think a hunk of rock spit him out full-grown. He was the orneriest, meanest old codger I've ever met," he said, chuckling as he shook his head in remembrance. "He gave me a job—out of the goodness of his heart, he said—then he worked my butt off. He wanted to grow potatoes in a field that was nine-tenths rock and one-tenth dirt. *Potatoes*," he said in disgust. "God made Idaho for potatoes. But Ephram wanted potatoes, so I broke my back moving those damn rocks. At first he didn't talk much. Oh, he mumbled a lot and cussed a blue streak, but he didn't really talk. Then after I'd been there about a month—that was before I got the Winnebago, so I lived with him in a decrepit old shack he called home—anyway, after I'd been there for a while he must have accepted me because every evening after dinner he'd light the worst-smelling cigar and we would talk." Tom turned his head to look at her, wonder filling his eyes. "Helen, you wouldn't believe the stories he told me. That cranky old man was a world traveler. Fifty years before he'd sailed the South China Sea. He was there when the Japanese seized Chinese provinces; he met Mao Tse-tung, who was then leading the Long March of his Red Army. At first I thought he was pulling my leg, but he knew just enough quirky details about the history and people in those parts to convince me that he was telling the truth." He closed his eyes. "The things he had seen, the people he had known . . . it was enough to boggle the mind."

"He sounds fascinating."

"He is. And he became a real friend. We still write. When I know I'll be someplace for a month or so, I send him a postcard with my new address." He laughed suddenly. "He's still complaining about the rocks I left in that field, when he knows damn well you'd have to use a microscope to find a rock there. He just doesn't want to admit he can't grow potatoes."

She laughed with him, then sighed in regret. "I hate to say it, but I think we'd better start back."

He sat up. "I was hoping you wouldn't notice how late it was."

"Don't you mean early? What time is it anyway?"

He peered at the luminescent dial of his watch. "Three."

She gasped. "You're joking!"

"I'm afraid not." He stared at her worried face. "Will you get expelled from Langston if they catch you?"

"I might. I don't know. I've never done anything like this before."

Reaching up, he touched the tip of her nose. "Do you regret it?"

"No," she whispered without hesitation. "No, I don't regret it."

His finger slid down to her lips, outlining them softly, then he drew it over her chin and down the long line of her throat. When it found the hollow between her breasts, he inhaled slowly and withdrew it.

"Not bulky or ugly enough," he muttered, then sat up. "You're right. We'd better go before I make a mistake and screw up our plans for tomorrow."

"Tomorrow?"

"It's my day off, remember? I thought we'd go on a picnic."

"Tom—" she said in confusion. "No, wait. I don't think I can—"

"Sure you can. All you have to do is say 'Yes, Tom, I'd love to go with you.' You see? Nothing simpler."

She laughed shakily. He made it sound easy, but he didn't know. Tonight a madness had struck her, a full-moon madness. Tomorrow it would be daylight, and everything would return to normal.

"Really, Tom—"

"Really, Helen," he whispered, leaning closer. "What could it hurt?"

What could it hurt? She almost laughed. Just knowing him, knowing he was near her each day, had disrupted her life enough. She felt threatened by the thought of letting him get closer. Moistening her lips nervously, she said, "I don't think—"

"That's right. Don't think," he whispered, the words a hot gust of air against her ear. "For once in your life don't think. Just feel."

He slid his hand under the black sweater, letting it come to rest below one breast. "Do you know what I wanted to do the first time I saw you?"

She cleared her throat. "You wanted to leave footprints on me?"

He chuckled softly, and the sound invaded her bloodstream, heating it. "No. I can't say that the idea of leaving a few fingerprints on you wasn't there, but mostly I wanted to see you stumble or sneeze—anything that was human. There was something in your eyes that I recognized. I had seen it in my own eyes. I wanted to grab you and say, 'It doesn't have to be there. You can change it,' but I knew you wouldn't have understood then." His hand slid around to her back, pulling her closer. "I think you can understand now. Don't shut me out. Don't shut the world out. Come with me tomorrow." He cupped her face, forcing her to look at him. "Nothing scary has happened tonight, has it?"

Helen shook her head even though she knew she was lying. There was something very scary happening inside her.

"Well, it could have. It's dark, and we're in a deserted spot. If I were going to harm you in any way I would have done it already. I knew you were unsure of me. That's why I haven't kissed you tonight. I didn't want to do anything to scare you off."

The heat of his hand against the flesh of her back was incredible. Glancing down, she saw his hand moving around to rest beneath her breast again.

"I want you to know I won't push you toward anything . . . physical."

Her indrawn breath was noisy to her own ears. "That's—that's very considerate of you."

"And sensitive," he said huskily as his thumb moved up to brush against her nipple. "Don't forget how sensitive I'm being to your feelings."

"You're—you're terrible," she whispered, backing away from him.

"Wait, don't pull away," he said urgently. When she continued to try to move away from him, he began to laugh. "Helen, I'm not being obstinate. My sleeve is caught."

She didn't trust him for a minute, but there did seem to be some kind of problem. "Close your eyes," she said cautiously.

Still chuckling, he did as she said. She lifted her sweater and sure enough, the frayed cuff of his shirt had caught in the front fastener of her bra. "How ridiculous," she muttered as she worked to free the fabric. "What if someone had come along? How on earth would we have explained this?"

"We could have said we were Siamese twins, joined at hand and breast," he offered. " 'We've considered surgery, but we're having too much fun.' "

"That's crude," she said, sputtering with laughter as she finally released his cuff. "Crude and insensitive."

He stood up, pulling her after him. "Nobody's perfect." He glanced down at her, and suddenly his eyes were pleading. "Tomorrow?"

If Helen went with him, she knew she would regret it. Maybe not right away, but sooner or later, she would regret it. Suddenly she didn't care. Staring at his face, she realized there was only one answer she could give him.

"Sure," she said as though it were inconsequential. "Sure," she repeated. "Why not?"

Four

Sunlight was streaming brightly through the sheer white curtains at the windows when Helen awoke the next morning. A smile tugged at the corners of her mouth as she rolled onto her side and rubbed her face against the pillowcase.

She felt wonderful—as if she wanted to get up and hug the world. She lay there for a moment, unable to remember why she felt so good. Then it came back to her. Tom. She laughed huskily. A wild midnight ride. A frog serenade.

Sitting up, Helen stretched luxuriously. When had she last felt so excited about simply waking up in the morning? she wondered happily. Not in years, she was sure. She was going on a picnic today. A picnic with Tom. Such a simple thing caused such euphoric reactions.

She jumped out of bed and inhaled deeply. The air smelled good. It felt good against her body. Stripping off her gown, she tossed it on the bed and headed for the bathroom. In the shower she rubbed her flesh vigorously, eagerly. Even her skin felt more alive than usual.

She chuckled as she dried off. If she had stopped to think about it, she would have been amazed at the sound of her own laughter. Helen was not one given to giggling in the bathroom—or anywhere else.

She was still smiling as she pulled slacks and a blouse from the closet. She couldn't get over how different she felt. The colors in her room and outside the window seemed brighter than usual.

Her fingers slowed in buttoning her blouse as a thought suddenly occurred to her. Maybe the day wasn't actually different from other days. Maybe she was simply more aware of things she normally took for granted.

She shook her head. Tom certainly seemed an unlikely sort of catalyst, but for her he was an effective one. She had the feeling that even when he was gone, when he moved on to his next stop, her life wouldn't settle into the same comfortable, boring rut that it had been in before. Tom's enthusiasm was contagious. Just being with him the night before had given her a new feel for life.

It was only as she was tucking in the bottom of a pale yellow blouse that she noticed that the loose, cotton trousers she had chosen were white. *White,* she thought, frowning, then quickly shrugged away the thought. It couldn't be helped. Most of her warm-weather things were white. She liked white. White suited her coloring, she decided stubbornly. And if Tom didn't like it, that was just too bad.

The telephone beside the bed rang, abruptly interrupting her almost belligerent thoughts. When she picked it up, her "Yes?" was just a little sharp.

"Mrs. Black is on the line," Terri replied, then added hesitantly, "I think she's been crying."

Helen frowned, concern for her friend growing in her blue eyes. "Put her on, Terri."

"Helen?" Charlotte's voice was quavery. "Helen, Brand left."

Helen felt her heart skip a beat. "Oh, Charlotte, I'm sorry."

Helen's concern was not without a touch of regret. Perhaps she should have made some kind of effort to warn Charlotte that a twenty-five-year-old man who spent most of his time in front of a mirror was not likely to spend the rest of his life with a plump, middle-aged divorcee—even if that divorcee was supporting him. Although Helen had felt anxious when her friend's affair began, she knew Charlotte had to live her own life, and so she had kept her doubts to herself.

"Helen, I feel so lost," Charlotte choked out. "I had planned my whole future around Brand."

"I know, I know," Helen murmured, her voice soothing. "Would you like me to come over? We could spend the day making fudge and ripping him apart. That always make you feel better."

"If I rip him apart, it will be with my bare hands." Charlotte's voice had lost its tragic tones and was filled now with healthy anger. "Helen, he said I was *fat*! Do you believe that? I can't count the number of times he told me that I was just the right size to fill his arms. He said he couldn't stand thin women. He said my breasts—"

"Charlotte," Helen interrupted. "I definitely do not want to hear what Brand said about your breasts. At least not before breakfast."

Her friend laughed, as Helen had known she would. Charlotte's sense of humor always managed to surface sooner or later.

"You're right," Charlotte said. "He's not worth talking about." She sighed. "Don't come over, Helen. I think I want to be alone. I know I'm a silly woman. I've always known it. And I guess down deep I've always known Brand would leave—like all the others left. But you see, I *hoped*. I always hope." She laughed again, but this time it was a terrible sound. "Hope is supposed to be such a wonderful thing. But it's not. It's a terrible emotion, ultimately debilitating. If I could just stop hoping, then maybe I could get on with my life and settle down to being alone."

Her voice dropped to a barely audible whisper. "I'm afraid of being alone, Helen. It's almost as though I don't exist unless there's someone beside me constantly telling me that I do. When there's a man in my life, I wake up in the morning smiling. There's something to get up for."

Helen inhaled slowly. Charlotte's confession disturbed her in more ways than she could admit at the moment. "I'm coming over, Charlotte," she said stubbornly. "You need someone to talk to."

"No, please don't. I want—I need to handle this

alone." She paused, and Helen was relieved to hear a smile in her voice again. "I know things can't be all bad when I've got friends like you."

Before Helen could respond, Charlotte said goodbye and hung up abruptly. She listened for a moment to the emptiness of the dial tone, then slowly replaced the receiver.

Helen rubbed her throbbing temples as she glanced at the clock on the nightstand. It was fifteen before nine. She had told Tom she would meet him at nine-thirty.

She stared out the window. Hadn't the sun been shining more brightly when she had awakened?

A picture of Tom flashed through her mind, and she heard Charlotte saying, "When there's a man in my life, I wake up in the morning smiling." It wasn't the same, she assured herself. Of course, it wasn't.

But she was afraid. She was afraid of making the same mistakes as her friend. Of being an object of ridicule. Of getting used to someone, then being left alone.

She couldn't go with him today. She would simply have to tell Tom she had changed her mind.

Helen felt as though a weight had been lifted from her shoulders. Of course, she couldn't go on a picnic. She had much more important things to do with her time.

When she left her bedroom and walked down the stairs, her steps were brisk. Tom would understand, she assured herself confidently. It wasn't as though she were about to break a date of long standing. The picnic was simply a spur of the moment idea conceived along with other fanciful thoughts under a full moon.

By the time she had finished picking at her breakfast, Helen was positive she had made the right decision. When she walked out onto the terrace there was an air of assurance about her. Then, without warning, Helen was lifted off her feet and swung into the air.

"A fair lady and a fair day," Tom said, grinning down at her stunned face. "What more could a man ask?"

"Tom!" she gasped, startled laughter making the word indistinct. "Put me down, you idiot."

"Nope," he said, stubbornly shaking his head. "You're my prize. My prize for being such an all-around good fellow." Suddenly he frowned as he studied what she was wearing. "Don't you own any jeans?"

"As a matter of fact, I don't." When Helen realized he was carrying her toward the Winnebago, she squirmed restlessly in his arms. "Tom, I can walk very well by myself. This is not necessary."

"Yes, it is necessary. When you came out of the house, you looked too dignified for words, and I felt that old urge to run through the snow." He set her down beside the motor home and smiled at her. "I had to shake up your dignity." He bowed. "Your chariot awaits."

She glanced warily at the motor home. "We're going in this?"

He grinned. "I didn't think you would feel comfortable on the motorcycle in broad daylight."

"That's an understatement. Half the town would

go into shock," she said wryly. "But the Winnebago is even worse. Everyone will see it as a mobile bed. And that will be the end of my carefully guarded reputation."

He raised one thick eyebrow. "I didn't know you were so close to being considered a fallen woman."

She shook her head in exasperation. "You know what I mean. People would talk."

The silence lengthened as he studied her face with obvious curiosity. "Don't you find that even a little amusing?" he asked. "Doesn't it make you want to ride through town and moon them or something?"

Helen choked on her stunned laughter. "No—no, I can't say that's my *immediate* reaction."

He threw his arms around her to give her a squeeze. "Don't worry about it. It would have come to you sooner or later." Releasing her, he stepped up into the Winnebago.

"I live in hope," she muttered, then blinked when he shoved a crumpled blanket into her arms.

"You carry that. I'll get the food into a basket," he said, his voice muffled because his head was inside a cabinet. "We'll take your convertible." He withdrew from the cabinet long enough to grin at her. "I'm not picky."

Fifteen minutes later they were on their way out of town, and Helen still couldn't understand how she came to be there. She remembered walking over to his mobile home to tell him she definitely wouldn't go with him. Everything after that was confusion. This man certainly had a way of turning her very thoughts upside down. Although she knew she should be annoyed that things hadn't turned out the way she had planned, she couldn't seem to drum up one ounce of irritation. The day was just too beautiful.

As they left the city limits behind, Helen began to notice her surroundings. On either side of the highway were fields of solid, brilliant color. The reds and yellows and purples of the wild flowers were spectacular. It was as though she had opened the farmhouse door and walked into the land of Oz.

It surprised Helen that Tom drove without consulting either a map or her. He seemed to know his way around very well and showed no hesitation as he took them to a wooded spot along a winding river.

"How long have you been in town?" she asked as they kneeled to spread the blanket on a grassy bank.

"Eight days."

She shook her head. "I've lived here more than twenty years. Why do you know this place when I've never seen it before?"

"You weren't looking," he said simply. "But that's all right. You're looking now."

She gazed out across the narrow, slow-moving river. "It's beautiful."

He flopped down on the blanket, then his eyes surveyed the area. "Yes, it's beautiful," he said quietly. "And as much as I respect Joe, no human hand is responsible for this. It's naturally beautiful, and there's order in the disorder. It's *right*."

He stretched in an unconsciously graceful movement and rolled over onto his side. The silence drew out comfortably as Helen looked at the stand of pines behind them, then the willows dotting the riverbank. From the corner of her eye she saw his reclining body. His jeans and T-shirt molded his body, showing hard, beautifully shaped muscles in his chest and thighs. Then suddenly Tom whispered, "Come here, Helen," and she jumped guiltily.

Pulling herself together, she moved to crouch beside him. After glancing at him in inquiry, she looked down to see what was holding his attention so thoroughly. A second later, she whispered, bewildered, "What are we watching?"

"Look closer."

She was in the mood to humor him, so she did as she was told. She stared down at the ground intently for a while, then said in exasperation, "Tom, there is nothing there but a lot of grass and sticks and—ouch!—*ants*. One of the little monsters bit me!"

"What did you expect? Your hand was right in the middle of his freeway," he said without looking up. "Watch them, Helen. Don't you see? They've got no time for gossip or backbiting. Hand-biting but not backbiting," he added, tongue in cheek. "They're doing what God put them here to do. Not one of them is worrying about what the other ants think of him."

Her expression was skeptical as she glanced first at Tom, then back to the ants. "How do you know that?" she said, her voice dry. "You see those two who are rubbing antennae so vigorously? They're probably saying, 'Did you *see* the weight Marian has put on? Don't let me get behind her in a tunnel; she's going to get stuck for sure.' "

He grinned in appreciation. "Don't you believe it. Ants are born knowing what's important. And wondering what their neighbors think of them is not on the list."

She started to argue with him, but stopped suddenly. "Oh, no!" she said. "Look at that caterpillar. He's headed right for the freeway." She leaned down. "Run for your lives. Godzilla's on the loose."

Tom shook with laughter as he pulled her closer. They watched as the fuzzy thing inched across blades of grass like a plump, awkward tightrope walker, each blade bowing down to give him access to the next blade.

"No sweat," Tom said after a moment. "I knew he'd never get there. He doesn't move in a straight line. He goes where the blades of grass take him."

Like you, she thought suddenly. Shaking away the disturbing thought, she rocked back on her heels and gave him a stern look. "Now I see. I knew you had an ulterior motive for this picnic. You wanted to get me out in the woods, away from civilization, away from all hope of rescue, to *watch bugs.*" She shook her head in regret. "How despicable."

He smiled. "It wasn't quite that bad. It's just that I've gotten very close to nature lately." He shrugged as though his motives made him a little uncomfortable. "I wanted to share it with you."

And share it he did. After they had eaten lunch they began to walk through the woods. Bugs had never been high on Helen's list of things of interest, but today she studied them. And birds. And plants. And tiny animals she would never have suspected lived in the underbrush.

"It's all natural," Tom said, his voice soft as though he were afraid of disturbing their surroundings. "I've met a lot of people in the last year who are like this. They don't need sleeping pills or tranquilizers. Hard work makes them sleep." He gazed out over the lazily moving river. "And the peace of nature is God's tranquilizer. Boredom doesn't exist. There is too much to do, too much to learn."

Helen considered his words as they walked down beside the river, peering into the shallow holes at schools of darting minnows. Tom's message wasn't all that subtle. She would have to be pretty dense to miss his point.

They were on a raised outcropping that overlooked a sluggish, shallow part of the river, when Helen glimpsed something shining in the murky water.

"Tom, look. I see something," she said. She leaned over to get a better look. When she saw what it was, she added, "Oh, never mind—"

The silk scarf that she wore draped around her neck slipped away. Before she could react, Tom grabbed at it. For a moment he seemed to be swimming in midair, then suddenly he was kneeling in mud and water. And in his hand was her scarf, held high out of harm's way.

For a moment Helen simply stood still, staring in stunned silence. Then as she examined the muddy water trailing down his face and chest, her lips began to quiver uncontrollably.

"Why, thank you, Tom," she choked out as she cautiously removed the scarf from his hand. "That was so gallant. Just like—just like Sir Walter Raleigh."

"What exactly were you trying to do?" he asked between clenched teeth.

The evil look in his eye was too much for her. She doubled over with laughter. She couldn't tell him that she had been trying to get a better look at the end of a beer can. And even if she had wanted to explain, she couldn't stop laughing to do so.

"You think that's funny, do you?" he asked quietly. He stood and slowly climbed the bank. Making sure she was watching, he bent down and scooped up a handful of mud. "Would you like to see something really funny?"

"No, Tom!" she gasped, still laughing as she backed away. "Now, be reasonable." She inched away from the dripping, oozing mass in his hand. "If our positions were reversed, you would laugh. You know you would."

His smile was devilish. "That doesn't—" He stopped abruptly, his eyes widening as he glanced over her shoulder. "Helen, stop!" he said urgently. "Look behind you."

She shook her head and kept backing up. "Oh, no. You're not going to get me with—"

Suddenly her feet went out from under her and the next thing Helen knew, she was sitting in the shallow muddy water. Feeling the water seep into her shoes was one of the oddest sensations she had ever experienced. Slowly, deliberately, she raised her gaze, staring up at him as though he were responsible. As she watched he dropped the mud, then raised his other hand to rub his chin, hiding his mouth in the process.

It didn't help. His eyes were laughing.

"You know—" He swallowed, then began again. "You know, you were right. I would laugh." He sat down on the bank and did just that.

It was only as he was helping her out that Helen began to laugh too. And once she started, she couldn't stop. Every time she glanced down at her once spotless white slacks or his streaked face, she began whooping again. For a long while they sat on the bank rocking back and forth in each other's arms, laughing.

After what seemed an hour Helen calmed down. Resting her chin in her palm, she stared up at him, her eyes sparkling with fun. "You really know how to give a girl a good time, don't you?"

He lifted a wet strand of her hair and grinned. "Actually I hadn't intended for us to study nature quite so closely." Rising to his feet in one fluid movement he reached down for her. "Come on, let's go get cleaned up."

She took his hand and let him pull her up, then followed as he walked beside the river. She hadn't given any consideration to how he meant to get them clean, so she was a little startled when he guided her to a clear wide spot in the river and, still holding her hand, stepped in.

"What are you doing?" she asked warily, trying to pull her hand out of his grasp.

"*We* are going to go in the river to wash the mud off our clothes," he said. When she still hesitated, he added, "Helen, there's not a single dry-cleaning establishment out here. Do you want to go home with mud all over you?"

"No," she said reluctantly, then she shrugged. "No, I guess I don't. Okay, let's get it over with."

She clenched her teeth and stepped in, then let out a startled yelp. The water was much deeper here and very cold. She waded out slowly until the water came up to her knees. She scowled at Tom, partly because it was his fault she was here and partly because the frigid temperature of the water seemed not to bother him at all.

He immediately began scooping up water and applying it to the mud on his clothes. Helen considered telling him what she thought of the false macho image that wouldn't let him squeal at walking into freezing water, but she decided the odds were ten to one that he wouldn't even know what she was talking about. She had a feeling his image was very real indeed. After a moment she shrugged and leaned over to mimic his movements.

Tom smiled as he watched her awkward splashing. "Here," he said, chuckling. "Let me help. You're missing most of it."

Stepping closer, he began smoothing water over the muddy streaks, then rubbing them gently. If he had ever envisioned the two of them being in such a predicament, he wouldn't have thought that Helen could be such a good sport about it. Maybe he had done her an injustice.

Suddenly his movements stopped, and he drew

in a sharp breath as he gazed down at her. The water had cleaned the mud from her clothes, all right, but in the process the fabric had become transparent. He swallowed hard. He would never again complain about her wearing white. The slacks were merely a clinging film about her lower body. He could see the pink flesh of her buttocks, and irresistibly his hands were drawn to her. He smoothed both palms over her perfectly formed bottom, finding joy in its shape. The yellow blouse clung to her back and he ran his hand up the long, visible line of her spine.

Helen stood still and silent beneath his intimate touch, but her breathing accelerated, and she felt the heat rise in her body. He turned her slowly and without a word began applying water to her legs, then to her stomach. His eyes shone as though lit with an inner fire; his hands shook as he cupped water and brought it to her breasts.

Helen's eyelids drifted down helplessly. Gently he shaped and squeezed each breast, his thumbs manipulating the taut nipples.

The silence between them was deafening. Then slowly she raised her eyelids and stared at him, her eyes glazed with desire. Bending slightly, she scooped up some water and smoothed it over his body. She kneaded the muscles in his upper arms, then ran her hands over his shoulder blades. The heat from his body warmed the water almost instantly as her hands moved across his wide chest, then his hard stomach, momentarily fondling his nipples and his navel. Kneeling in the water, she placed one hand on either side of his right thigh and let the water trickle downward. Then, ignoring his hoarse gasp, she did the same to the left thigh.

Inhaling audibly, he reached down to pull her to her feet. For long, electrically charged moments he simply stared into her eyes, then with agonizing slowness he lowered his lips to hers. As their bodies came together the warmth of their flesh merged; they might as well have been naked.

Neither of them spoke when the kiss ended. As they gazed into each other's eyes there was a kind of peace between them, as though a deep, silent agreement had been reached. Arm in arm, they started out of the water.

Before they reached the bank, Helen paused, looked up at Tom, and laughed. He stared at her lovely face and smiled. "Are you laughing at me, madam?" he asked sternly.

She shook her head. "No." She wrapped her arms around his waist, leaning her head back so she could see his face. "I'm laughing because"— she inhaled exuberantly—"because the sun is shining. Because the birds are singing." She stood on tiptoe to dust a fleeting fairy kiss across his lips. "Because I'm happy."

That was enough explanation for Tom. It was all that mattered at that moment. They were together and they were happy being together. They had taken the first step.

At least that was how it felt to him. But later on the drive home Tom began to wonder if he had been mistaken. He could feel a change coming over Helen. With each mile she withdrew from him further. It was such a subtle change, at first he wondered if it were his imagination. But when she turned and smiled that practiced smile, he knew he was right.

"Joe tells me your daughter's baby is due in three months," he said, somehow feeling conversation was necessary now. "How do you feel about becoming a grandmother?"

"I'm looking forward to it," she said, her voice polite. A car passed them, coming from the direction of Langston, and she leaned forward to adjust her shoe.

He frowned at her action but didn't remark on it. "And how does Audrey feel about being a mother?" Talking to her now was like walking through molasses.

"She's thrilled. I just hope—" She broke off as though she regretted having spoken.

"You hope?" he urged, keeping his voice even with effort. He was beginning to get annoyed. They had just shared something wonderful, and she was acting as though they were strangers.

"Nothing really," she said, shrugging away his question. "Audrey and her husband are having a few small problems. But I'm sure things will work themselves out when the baby arrives."

"I'm sure," he murmured. He tightened his fingers on the steering wheel. How long would it be before she stopped fighting him? He glanced at her. Even in those damp, disreputable-looking clothes, she seemed untouchable. "Helen," he said softly. "What happened?"

She turned to stare at him. "I'm sorry," she said in confusion. "I don't know what you mean."

And she didn't. He was almost sure she had no idea what he was talking about. The thought saddened him immeasurably. At first Tom had felt only an unexplainable need to bring Helen back to life, to crack her elegant shell. But now there was more. He didn't know where the relationship would lead—if it was, in fact, a dead end. He only knew he wanted to be close to her now, close to the Helen who had stood in the river and opened her heart to him.

Five

"No, no, *no!*"

Helen glanced at Charlotte and rolled her eyes as Althea Phillips paced in front of them on the stage, taking her role as director as an excuse to lecture vigorously. They were in the final stages of rehearsal for the women's club musical, and as usual tempers were running high.

This year they were offering their own version of Gilbert and Sullivan's *The Mikado*. Helen chuckled softly. There was not a professional among them, and as a result rehearsals were often chaotic. But they had fun, and it was for a good cause.

One of the charter members, Helen took pride in the women's club. She liked the musicals and the charity balls, but even more she liked the good the club did for the people of Langston and the surrounding county. They made very real contributions to the town with the money raised by various events. The Christmas ball two years earlier had paid for new equipment for the hospital. Helping Heart, a refuge for abused women and children, was almost entirely funded by the club. And through their efforts, there were occasional concerts and art exhibits that otherwise wouldn't have come to such a small town.

They had just finished running through the "Three Little Maids from School" number for the sixth time. Helen, Charlotte, and Barbara Ludlow, who played the third Little Maid, were in the center of the stage. Although they were all dressed in casual clothes, each carried a large fan, a prop that was necessary to the movements during the song.

"Charlotte," Althea continued, "I don't know where your mind is"—she glanced at the darkly tanned young man slumping lazily in one of the first-row seats as though she knew very well where Charlotte's mind was—"but you simply must concentrate on the song. Think of the motivation, dear," she added, her voice dripping with sarcasm. "I'm sure if you could somehow manage to understand that, it would help us all tremendously."

Charlotte leaned closer to Helen, her vibrant red curls bouncing wildly as though they shared her indignation, and whispered, "What do you want to bet that next time she tries to make me stand in the corner? Who elected her dictator anyway?"

" 'Think of the motivation, dear,' " Helen mimicked, holding the wide fan up to cover her lips lest Althea's wrath fall on her next. "She certainly makes me feel like I'm still in school."

When Charlotte expressed her feelings by crossing her eyes, Barbara giggled helplessly, bringing Althea's attention back to them all.

"*If* you three are quite ready?" she asked, raising one thin eyebrow in haughty inquiry. After a moment she turned to face the skeleton orchestra in the pit. "Let's start that one over again."

As soon as Althea turned away, Helen shook her head and whispered, "I still can't understand how she managed to get the director's job."

Charlotte smiled wickedly. "In true show-business tradition, Althea used her body to get her position. She threatened to strip down in front of the sponsors if they didn't appoint her director."

Barbara gave a loud yelp of laughter, then hastily turned it into a cough when Althea glared at her. Needless to say, the beginning of their number was a little shaky, and Helen had to avoid Charlotte's eyes in order to continue.

Later as she waited for her next number, Helen watched Charlotte flirt with her new "friend," but her mind kept sliding back to Tom. She had looked such a mess when they had returned from their picnic last week. She'd felt painfully self-conscious but exhilarated too. He couldn't know just how much she had enjoyed their outing.

She smiled, remembering the way she had sneaked into the house on their return, carrying her soggy shoes, tiptoeing like a teenager out past curfew. She had considered herself very lucky that no one had been around, because a reasonable explanation for the condition of her clothes would have been beyond her.

Suddenly her brow creased as she thought of the

way Tom had acted on the drive home that day. Some kind of barrier had come up between them, and his silence had worried her until they met again the next day. When she had found no constraint between them, she had decided her imagination was working overtime.

Since then Helen had managed to spend more and more of her time inspecting her grounds. After all, she told herself righteously, it was spring. Naturally she would be interested in how her gardens were growing.

Helen almost laughed aloud. Whom was she trying to fool? There was only one thing in her garden that held her interest, and it definitely wasn't petunias. She was constantly drawn to Tom's side. And when she was near him, the world sparkled.

"Well, what do you think?"

Helen blinked in confusion, then turned to find Charlotte sitting beside her. "I'm sorry, Charlotte," she said. "What did you say?"

"I asked how you liked him." She nodded toward the young man who was now striding toward the exit. "Isn't he positively gorgeous?"

"He's very attractive," Helen agreed slowly. "But don't you think he's a little too . . . too athletic?"

She had almost said too young, and that was one thing Charlotte didn't need to hear. Helen had worried over her friend's depression after Brand had departed. She couldn't help thinking that another young, thoughtless man wasn't the answer for her friend. But Helen had been almost thankful to see Charlotte with a new man today. At least Charlotte had something to take her mind off her loneliness.

"Athletic?" Charlotte said with a mischievous grin. "Yes, he's that all right. And he's not bad out of bed either." She wiggled her eyebrows. "Didn't I tell you he's the new racquetball instructor at the country club? I met him when I signed up for lessons."

"You're taking racquetball lessons?" Helen asked, her eyes widening skeptically. Charlotte was the least athletic person she knew. "Since when have you been interested in sports?"

"Since they hired a new instructor," she said blithely, then leaned closer. "His name is Rocky. Do you believe that?" She grimaced. "He also lifts weights, and he's—how shall I put it?—he's a diamond in the rough. But he's so cute, I don't even mind about the weights."

Suddenly the redhead's expression changed, becoming more serious. "Helen, he's so special. I've never met anyone like him. I want to be with him every minute. And I feel more alive than I have in years." She laughed. "He wants to take care of me. Isn't that a kick?" Charlotte was trying very hard to sound amused, but her voice quivered, and there was a faraway look in her eyes as she murmured, "I think . . . I really think this is finally it for me."

Oh, Charlotte, Helen thought. Please don't get hurt again. How could she keep this up? Couldn't Charlotte see that she was only letting herself in for the same heartbreak all over again? Why did she always have to depend on a man for her emotional stability? Helen wondered.

Helen was still worrying about Charlotte when she left the theater later. But slowly thoughts of Charlotte and Althea and the musical slid away, and there was room in her mind only for Tom. As she pictured his laughing face, her muscles began to relax. It was as though they were suddenly freed of some kind of restraint. The sensation was incredibly satisfying. And she knew Tom was responsible; she simply couldn't understand why.

She smiled. He would be surprised to know that his lectures had taken effect. Of course, she would never tell him. He was much too sure of himself as it was. Helen wasn't about to give him more ammunition.

She stopped the car at a red light, drumming her fingers against the steering wheel as she thought of the evening ahead. He had invited her to dinner in his Winnebago, and the meal promised to be quite an experience, an unconventional sort of date. But then, she mused, Tom was an unconventional sort of man.

He was such a puzzle, she thought. He was intelligent, articulate, and sharp-witted. It seemed wrong somehow that he should be a drifter.

Suddenly she frowned. Would she feel the same freedom with him if he were a businessman like her late husband's friends? Would she be as eager to see him if they were dining in her home or at a restaurant in town? She shook her head. No, it wouldn't be the same at all. She wouldn't feel as free. It was best that he was just as he was, she decided as she continued the drive home.

At seven-thirty that evening Arnold brought the

car around to the front of the house for her. It was difficult for Helen to keep a straight face as she airily waved good-bye to Patty and Arnold, then simply drove around the block to the back entrance, parking the car so it would be hidden from view by the Winnebago.

Tom appeared beside the car instantly, opening the door for her. "Are you sure you weren't followed?" he whispered urgently.

Helen glanced nervously over her shoulder. She started to speak, then she saw his sparkling eyes. "You're laughing," she accused.

"Of course, I am," he said. "Don't you think it's a little ridiculous to drive to your own backyard?"

She stared at him for a moment, then she, too, began to laugh. "Yes, I guess it is. I just couldn't think of any other way to get here without answering a lot of questions. If I had simply told Patty I didn't want dinner tonight, she would have insisted on calling the doctor."

He smiled. "It really doesn't matter how you got here, just as long as you're here." He motioned to the door. "Won't you step into my parlor?"

"As a matter of fact, you do look a little spiderish tonight," she said, eyeing his black slacks and black shirt as she passed him.

"The better to bite you, my dear."

She chuckled, glancing slowly around his home. It wasn't exactly roomy, but it looked comfortable. Every available inch of space was put to use. On one side of the mid-section was the kitchen counter with sink, built-in range, and refrigerator. On the other were two doors which she assumed led to a bathroom and closet. The front contained driver and passenger bucket seats, a dining alcove, and a couch. And although she didn't care to inspect it too closely, the back of the vehicle seemed to contain nothing more than wall-to-wall bed.

Helen glanced up to find Tom watching her. "Well, what do you think of my humble abode?" he said, studying her face intently.

"It's amazing." She gestured around them. "It has so much packed into so little space, yet it doesn't make you feel claustrophobic."

He nodded. "A product of modern ingenuity. Not an inch of wasted space. The couch and table, for instance, convert to extra beds. So handy for impromptu orgies," he said, leaning toward her to twist wickedly at an imaginary mustache. Then he nodded toward the couch. "Sit down and I'll fix us drinks. I suppose you prefer white wine? If not, I also have beer and grape Kool-Aid."

She laughed. "As a matter of fact, I love white wine. And no comments about the color, please." She sniffed the air. "Something smells good. What are we having?"

He smiled smugly. "Would you believe chicken Kiev?"

She whistled in admiration, giving him the tribute he obviously expected. "I'm very impressed. That just happens to be one of my favorite dishes."

"I know," he said, his grin looking amazingly boyish. "I asked Patty."

For a moment she remained silent, her eyes growing suspicious, then she said, "And I suppose she also gave you the recipe?"

"Well . . . to tell the truth Patty prepared it." His chagrin at being found out was patently false, and Helen wasted no time in telling him so.

"You're terrible," she said, shaking her head.

He raised his wineglass, acknowledging the truth of her statement. "I really didn't go begging," he explained. "In the course of a perfectly ordinary conversation I happened to mention that I was having company for dinner. I told her I wanted to make something really special and asked what you preferred. I told Patty I thought it was safe to use your tastes as a standard of gentility."

"And you've got more blarney in you than a County Cork leprechaun," she said. "I suppose you gave her your sad-eyed look, and she offered to prepare dinner for you." She sent him a shaming glance. "I know Patty. She's a sucker for a sad tale. I guess she should consider herself lucky you didn't need money. She would have cashed in her savings bonds without batting an eyelash. You're really something."

"Can I help it if I was born with more charm than the average man?" he said guilelessly. "She said I reminded her of her first husband."

Helen stared at him for a moment; then she began to laugh in genuine amusement.

"What's so funny?"

She shook her head helplessly. "She's told me about her first husband," she said, still chuckling. "He spent more time in jail than he did with Patty. I think his family threw a celebration party when he got run over by a truck—right after he had swindled several little old ladies out of their life savings."

For a moment he tried to look offended, but he couldn't maintain his sober expression for long and grinned appreciatively. "I'll get her for that," he said amiably as he turned to take their dinner out of the oven.

Throughout dinner, with candles flickering on the table and Edith Piaf singing huskily in the background, the laughter and the talk continued. Helen had not talked—talked and really said something—in years. Not since her early college days when she was still riding high on youthful enthusiasm. No subject seemed too trivial for them to explore and compare thoughts on.

When the dishes had been cleared, Helen reached across the table to pick up the half-full wine bottle. As she poured she murmured, "I can't figure you out. You're one of the most intelligent men I've ever met, but you simply drift around from one job to another. Haven't you ever wanted to make something of yourself? Haven't you ever wanted to do something—oh, I don't know—something worthwhile?"

He raised a single brow, a crooked smile spreading across his strong lips. "Worthwhile," he murmured. "Now I wonder what your definition of *worthwhile* is? I have a horrible feeling it's different from mine." He shrugged. "Johnny Appleseed did what I'm doing. Do you consider his life worthwhile? What about Thoreau?"

She laughed softly, unaware that the atmosphere between them had undergone a subtle change. "You put yourself in the same category as Thoreau?" she asked, resting her chin in her palm to study him.

He stared down at the glass in his hand and then suddenly looked up, a strange expression on his face. "Maybe not," he said softly. "But then you wouldn't be here with me if I weren't what I am." His smile was a little sad now. "I'm something along the lines of forbidden fruit, aren't I?"

She set her glass down, the expression on her face revealing the confusion she was feeling. "No—no, you're twisting everything. It isn't like that at all." She rubbed her temple. "I admit that I experience a certain sense of freedom when I'm with you, but it's nothing illicit like you're making it out to be."

He leaned back in his seat, exhaling slowly. "I'm simply stating the facts as I see them. You refuse to have anything to do with the men in your own social sphere." When she glanced at him sharply, he added, "Oh, yes. I've watched you. The night of your dinner party you were in the garden with a real nice-looking guy. You talked casually at first, but when you stopped walking and leaned up against a tree, he took it as an invitation." He smiled grimly. "You froze him dead. The poor guy looked like a train had derailed on top of him." He shook his head as though regretting the necessity of his words. "All night I watched you giving the men around you that polite, sterile grimace that's supposed to be a smile. And to tell you the truth, it made me sick."

How dare he, Helen fumed silently. He had spied

on her. And he admitted it, as though it weren't a thoroughly despicable act. She was furious with him, and she didn't bother to hide it. "So you watched me—*spied* on me," she said tightly. "So I wouldn't allow a man to paw me in the garden. What is that supposed to prove?"

He leaned forward, resting his forearms on the table. "You've allowed me to 'paw' you several times. Why?"

"Because I couldn't stop you," she ground out. "Because you have the manners of a jackass."

"You could be right about my manners, but I don't think that's the reason. I think you let it happen because I'm not permanent." When she moved to stand, he grabbed her wrist. "No, you're going to listen to the truth for once. I think you let it happen because someday soon I'll move on. Then you'll be able to get on with your nice, comfortable, sterile life." He glanced down at her arm, then very deliberately dropped it. Leaning back, he examined her thoroughly and critically. "You seek me out and let me touch you in any way I want, always confident that your bed will stay as pristine as the clothes you wear." He laughed harshly. "No one is allowed to rumple the Snow Queen's sheets."

She gasped and rose abruptly. "That's enough. You have no right to say that."

"Maybe not, but it's the truth." He stood also, but only to push her down onto the couch. He leaned close to examine her face. "Do you even remember what a bed looks like after two people have made love in it?" His voice dropped to a raspy whisper. "Do you remember what *you* look like after you've been loved? It's not neat, Helen. It's not orderly. Your hair is tangled and damp." His breath was hot on her cheek, adding to the intensity of his words. "Your body is all slick and shiny with perspiration. Your lips are swollen . . . and your breasts—"

He barely paused when he heard her strangled protest. He didn't take his eyes from her flushed face. It was as though he knew what he was doing to her.

"Your breasts are swollen, too, Helen," he continued without mercy. "They're full and throbbing, the nipples sore from my fingers, my teeth. You'll smell my scent on your skin. And down between your thighs—"

"No!" She barely got the word out. With the strength born of fear Helen jerked away from him, standing and moving swiftly toward the door, desperately afraid he would stop her, afraid of what would happen if he did.

But he didn't even try, and she paused at the door. *"You stay away from me,"* she bit out. "I don't want to see you again. Not until I see your back as you leave."

Without waiting for his reaction, she stepped out and stumbled toward the house. She didn't care if anyone saw her return. She just wanted to get away from him. Her movements were awkward as she rushed through the empty rooms, running as though all the demons of hell were after her.

In the darkness of her bedroom she fumbled frantically with the lock and then turned to slump weakly against the door. But the door proved to be a poor barrier. It couldn't lock out what was inside her.

For a long time she stayed there, waiting for her heart to stop pounding. When at last she moved, she didn't turn on the light. She was afraid of what she would see on her own face in the mirror. As she walked slowly toward the bathroom, each step seemed somehow painful.

The large bathroom was lined with mirrors, and Helen could see her ghostly form moving in the dark, but still she didn't touch the light switch. She showered in the dark, scrubbing her flesh, punishing it for being on fire from his words.

Her movements were jerky as she pulled on a pale peach gown and began to pace her bedroom. No sleep, she thought feverishly. There would be no sleep for her tonight.

Why had it happened? When had things fallen apart? In the beginning the evening had been one of the nicest she could remember. Then somehow the fabric of their empathy had become twisted and tangled.

Suddenly the air around her felt stifling. She walked across the room and threw open the door to the balcony. Bright moonlight struck her with almost physical force. Nothing was gentle tonight, Helen told herself.

Her eyes were irresistibly drawn across the broad expanse of lawn to the motor home, then she sucked in a sharp breath. He was there, standing motionless in the moonlight. And although she couldn't see his eyes, she knew they were trained on her. For an endless moment she was held in the grip of his gaze, and the heat inside her grew unbearably. Then without warning, he was gone.

She sagged weakly against the wall. Why was he doing this to her? Why was she *allowing* him to do this to her? she wondered in despair. He was her gardener, for heaven's sake. He was nothing to her and never would be. She didn't want to see him ever again.

Then with a painful sigh Helen admitted the truth to herself at last. If he climbed the trellis tonight, they would make love. There was no doubt about it. The desire between them was too strong for it to be otherwise.

But he wouldn't. She had seen his eyes as he spoke. There was desire there, but beneath the desire had been contempt. He was punishing her for what she was.

She wrapped her arms around her body, rocking gently, trying to soothe the terrible need she felt. Tears of frustration pooled in her eyes, and she wiped at them mechanically. Then her hand dropped to cover her lips—to stop something. A groan, a scream, it didn't matter what it was. She knew she had to stop it. She had to stay calm. The pain would pass soon. No one could bear this kind of torment for long.

Turning, she stepped toward the door. Then abruptly her movements were halted by the sound of rustling leaves. Her breath caught in her throat; her nails dug into her forearms; slowly she turned around.

Tom was standing not three feet from her. His eyes were a dark blaze in the moonlight, his hair disheveled as though he had run frustrated fingers through it again and again. Helen stared at him in strained silence, unaware of how much of her inner struggle was revealed in her face.

When he spoke at last, the words were barely audible. "I sounded pretty condemning before, didn't I?"

She nodded jerkily.

He stepped closer. "I had no right. I don't allow you to question my life. I have no right to criticize yours." He inhaled, and the indrawn breath sounded painful. "I was simply using anger to hide the real problem. The need, Helen." He ran his fingers through his hair as though he were stalling for time to find the right words. "If we two—different as we obviously are—can find common ground, why should we spoil it with questions?"

She shook her head, not because she disagreed with him, but because she couldn't take in his words. She couldn't get past the fact that he was here. He was really here.

Again he stepped closer, and, as though it had a will of its own, her body swayed toward him, her eyes closing weakly. He raised his hand to touch her shoulder. It was a small movement, the lightest of touches, but Helen bit her lower lip to keep from moaning.

His mouth was against her ear when next he spoke. "This is a beautiful gown, Helen." His voice sounded hoarse as though he had to force his vocal cords to work. "But I don't want to feel silk. I want to feel *you*."

She experienced the same light touch on her

other shoulder. Then with a whisper of silk, the gown slid down her body and the moonlight struck her flesh.

"I want to love you, Helen. May I?"

She made a small sound at the back of her throat. It wasn't a moan exactly; it was the sound of an animal in pain. She felt weak and suddenly didn't know if she had the strength to stand. She knew he wouldn't make another move until she made a conscious decision.

Raising her hand, she touched his face and leaned her body into his. *"Please,"* she whispered huskily.

The breath left Tom's body in a harsh gust when he heard her soft plea. For a few brief seconds he felt that his legs would give way, then holding her hand tightly, he turned and led her inside to the bed. Hesitating for only a moment, he began to unbutton his shirt.

As he removed his clothes Helen couldn't take her eyes off him. She felt no shyness, no embarrassment, perhaps because her need was so great, it overrode every other emotion.

Raising her hand slowly, she reached out to touch his bare chest. And it was only when she felt him tremble beneath her fingers that she realized Tom was as vulnerable as she was. It gave her the confidence to reach down and help him unzip his slacks.

When he at last stood naked beside her, Tom had to exert maximum control on his emotions. He wanted to throw her on the bed and show her how wildly his desire had grown out of control in the past few weeks. But he also wanted this night to be special for both of them. He had waited too long to make a mistake now.

Raising his hands, he let them come to rest on her rib cage then drift slowly down her body. The filtered moonlight struck her creamy flesh and her beauty took his breath away.

"You're even more lovely than I imagined," he whispered. When she moaned and pressed her lower body against his, he exhaled shakily. "Helen, you're going to have to help me. I want to take it slow for you, but"—he grasped her shoulders and held her away from him—"but I can't when you move your hips like that."

She gave a breathless laugh when she heard the helpless frustration in his voice. Standing on tiptoe, she found his earlobe with her lips. "I don't need it slow, Tom," she murmured huskily. "Not this time. I need you. I need you on top of me. I need you hard and fast. I need you any way I can get you."

"My God!" he rasped out. Their descent to the bed was less than graceful, but it was totally satisfying.

His hands searched her body feverishly, learning the angles and curves, the peaks and valleys, as though he felt the need to reassure himself that she was truly there on the bed beneath him. This time he didn't try to stop her when she began moving against him, but merely moaned in pleasure-pain as the heat of her body reached him.

When he touched the heated spot between her thighs, she parted her legs, urging him into her with short, breathy words of encouragement. A moaning sigh escaped her when she felt the full length of him inside her. Without pause he began to love her.

He gave her everything she had asked for—and more. And he took everything she had to give—and more. He made love to her with a hunger that went deep and took a lot of loving to assuage. And Helen welcomed each hard stroke because she had a lot of loving to give.

The climax of their passion was spectacular, bursting inside Helen's mind and body like whirling colored rockets. It took her out of herself to a place made for them alone.

When her breathing returned to normal, Helen lay there for long moments, absorbing the beauty of what had just happened to her. A strange feeling came over her, and, as though she had moved outside her body, she observed the two people on her bed.

Everything he had said was true. It wasn't neat. The satin sheets were twisted beneath them and hanging untidily off the side of the bed. Her hair was tangled and damp around her face. Leaning her head to the side, she pressed her face to her own shoulder and found the scent of him on her flesh. She touched her breasts, and a thrill shot through her as she felt their soreness. Her body was covered with a slick film of perspiration.

No, it wasn't neat, Helen mused, but it was the most exciting thing that had ever happened to her. What had he done to her to make her feel so bonelessly wonderful? No one had ever moved her so completely. She felt so much a woman. And it was all due to this man beside her.

When she thought of the wild range of emotions she had experienced that night, Helen knew she had much to be grateful for. Even the deep pain she had felt before he came to her was welcome in retrospect. It meant she was alive, truly alive for the first time in years.

Reaching out, she touched his chest, learning the muscles, the bones, the tendons. She felt the beat of his heart, then let her hand slide down to his manhood and cradled him there as though she could discover the essence of him.

"Helen, Helen," he murmured, his mouth pressed hotly against her neck. "Are you some kind of witch? Five minutes ago you took my strength; you drained me of everything. Now you're giving it back again." He turned his head to stare into her eyes. "Witch," he whispered again. "Beautiful, beautiful witch." Then he moved above her to love her once again.

Helen awoke in the middle of the night to find Tom leaning over her. "I've got to leave now, love," he said softly. "It will be daylight soon."

Sleepily she raised her arms to clasp them around his neck. "I don't want you to go," she murmured, her voice husky. "The bed will be so empty."

"My arms too. But the sun won't wait for us." He kissed her deeply, then loosened her arms and turned to the balcony door.

"Wait," she said, sitting up. "You don't have to climb down. I'll let you out and lock up behind you."

He laughed softly. "That's much too mundane an ending for a night of magic." He shook his head. "No, love, let's keep this fairytale night perfect." And then, blowing her a kiss, he slipped through the door.

Six

It was the day of Helen's annual garden party. The back lawn was awash with billowing pastel chiffon and wide-brimmed matching hats. From the landscaped terrace to the sparkling pool at the side of the house, clusters of people gathered. Each year they came from all over Texas to worship spring and more recently to celebrate the success of the yearly musical production.

The caterer's helpers, wearing pristine white coats, moved efficiently among the guests. A small, tuxedo-clad orchestra was stationed to one side of the terrace, providing soft background music by Strauss and Vivaldi. Later on, after her guests had had a few drinks, the music would change by request. The orchestra was prepared. They could play anything from Glenn Miller to Bob Wills to Stevie Wonder. It was the same every year.

Dressed from head to toe in mint green, Helen looked cool and collected as she circulated among her friends and neighbors. Only those who knew her intimately were able to guess that her thoughts weren't completely given over to her guests. Lately her thoughts had been dominated by one person. One man.

In the weeks since that first wonderful night she and Tom had been together as much as possible. Not that Helen neglected her club duties or her other activities, but she always found herself impatient to get back to Tom. She felt whole when she was with him. Although he no longer complained about her clothes, he still teased her and called her the Snow Queen.

By unspoken agreement they kept their relationship secret, each for his or her own reason. And in some ways the secret bound them even tighter. By day she was his employer and by night she was his lover.

She smiled contentedly, then glanced around the terrace. She waved when she saw Chad and Audrey beside a temporary bar. Apparently they had just arrived. As she studied them fine lines of worry appeared around her eyes. They were arguing again. Helen had hoped that after her talk with Chad, they would manage to straighten things out. It wasn't good for either of them to live under constant strain. She moved swiftly to them, hugging each in turn.

"I'm so glad you could come," she said, including them both in her smile.

"It's good to see you, Helen," Chad said, returning her smile.

"Oh, we wouldn't have missed it, would we, darling?" Audrey asked, her voice heavy with sarcasm. "Just think of all the business contacts Chad can make."

Audrey glanced at Chad, but he didn't seem to notice Audrey's cynical comment. He was searching the clusters of people scattered around the garden.

"There's Mr. Nicholson," he said to Audrey. "I'd better go touch base." Glancing back at his wife, he added, "Remember to spend some time with his wife."

"You can tell his wife to go—"

But Chad was already gone, and Audrey stopped in frustration. She turned to her mother. "You see what I mean? I don't count with him anymore. He doesn't even hear what I say."

Helen stared after her son-in-law. "I can't understand it. Chad is usually so sensitive and thoughtful. How can he let this trouble between you continue when the doctor has said you should avoid stress?"

When her daughter avoided her eyes, Helen said sharply, "Audrey? What's going on? Surely you told him what the doctor said?"

The younger woman sighed heavily. "I don't want to blackmail him into loving me, Mother. Or into needing me. Can't you see?" she asked, her voice intense. "I don't want him to stay home with me because of my health. I want him to be there because he wants to be there."

Helen shook her head, her eyes worried. "You're taking an awful chance, Audrey. You should be thinking of your health and the baby's." When her daughter's expression remained stubborn, Helen said, "Look, I've been thinking about what he told me the night of my dinner party, and I believe I know what's driving Chad."

Audrey pulled off her hat and held it against her enlarged middle. Her hair was a shade darker than Helen's and looked like golden honey in the sunlight. "Well, I wish you would tell me," she said irritably. "I'm beginning to think that the man I sleep with—and I do mean *sleep* with—is someone pretending to be the man I married."

"I think Chad is afraid."

"Of what? Of not being voted apple-polisher of the year?" she asked dryly.

Helen gave her daughter a warning glance. "Do you want my opinion or not?"

"I'm sorry, Mother." She shifted uncomfortably under her mother's disapproval. "This thing is driving me crazy. What is Chad afraid of?"

Helen gazed at her for a moment and then said quietly, "I think he's afraid of losing you."

Audrey's eyes opened wide as she stared across the lawn at her husband. There wasn't any cynicism in her expression now, merely yearning. Then she slowly shook her head. "If he were afraid of losing me he wouldn't be ignoring me." She glanced up. "What makes you say that anyway? I'm not the one who spends all my time away from home."

Helen hid a wry smile. "I don't know if I've mentioned this before, my darling daughter, but I'm afraid you're just a wee bit spoiled."

"You've mentioned it," Audrey said, rolling her

eyes. "I'm not admitting anything, you understand, but on the slight possibility you're right, what does that have to do with what's going on?"

Helen reached out to smooth back a strand of her daughter's hair. "He said there were things that he wanted to give you, things you would expect when the excitement of marriage wore off."

"Excitement?" she said, staring in exaggerated astonishment. "Marriage hasn't been exciting since I started resembling an oil tanker."

"You know what I mean," Helen said, chuckling.

Her daughter nodded reluctantly. "And what does he think I'll expect?"

"The things you've always had," Helen said, shrugging slightly. "Vacations in Europe. Shopping trips to New York. Designer clothes. An expensive home in which to entertain your friends. Servants."

Audrey closed her eyes, but not before Helen had seen the guilt there. After a moment her daughter said quietly, "I just want Chad." She inhaled deeply. "What you've said may be the excuse he's giving himself to justify his neglect. But I don't think the answer is that simple."

Helen ached for her daughter. She wanted to help and briefly wished for the days when making it all better was as simple as a kiss or a chocolate cupcake. "Will you talk to him about it at least?"

"All I ever do is talk to him about it," she said shortly. Then when she caught Helen's eyes, she smiled wearily. "Yes, I'll talk to him. Now let's go find some food. I'm starving . . . as usual." Suddenly she frowned. "Uh-oh. You're being stalked.

Althea Phillips and Charlotte are converging upon you from different directions. Sorry to desert you, but Althea gives me a pain. Tell Charlotte hi for me."

Helen watched her daughter duck into a small group, helplessly wishing she, too, could run, but Althea was already upon her.

"Helen, my dear, you've outdone yourself. This will be your best garden party ever."

Helen smiled. "You tell me that every year, Althea," she was saying as Charlotte joined them.

"I don't think anyone's even noticed that the salmon is just a wee bit off," the thin brunette continued, ignoring Charlotte's arrival.

"You say *that* every year too," Charlotte muttered.

Whether she had intended it or not, Charlotte immediately drew Althea's fire away from Helen. "Charlotte dear, what a lovely outfit." Althea ran her gaze slowly over the wildly printed fabric of Charlotte's jump suit as she smoothed down the skirt of her own muted lavender dress. "And how brave of you to wear that color with your hair."

Before Charlotte could say what was on the tip of her tongue, Helen jumped in. "You do look lovely, Charlotte. I like your new hairstyle."

"Thank you, Helen," she said, inhaling deeply. "I've got a new hairdresser. You should try him, Althea. He can work wonders with the most unmanageable hair."

"Why, you—"

"I haven't seen Rocky," Helen asked quickly. "He came with you, didn't he?"

Charlotte nodded. "He's hot on the trail of a tray of canapés," she said, grinning indulgently. "He's so sweet, Helen. Last night he took me out to dinner to celebrate my part in *The Mikado*. I wore that blue outfit I bought last week when we went shopping."

Althea smiled thinly. "How wonderful for you, darling. I do hope you were careful. I don't think Secret Sauce comes out of silk."

Charlotte laughed in surprise, then looked at Althea appreciatively. "Very good, Althea. That was extremely subtle." She reached up to push back her hat as though preparing for battle. "I myself prefer to be blunt. Rocky may not have your Ronald's class, but at least he knows that foreplay doesn't refer to golf."

Helen gasped. "Have you noticed how beautiful the flowers are this year?" she said urgently, trying with difficulty to keep a straight face.

Charlotte grinned and looked around the garden. "I haven't paid attention to the flowers, but I definitely have noticed the new gardener." She sighed dreamily. "He's such a hunk, Helen. Where did you find him?"

"You've met Tom?"

"I've seen him in town. I asked Mr. Evans at the nursery who he was and nearly fainted when he told me he was working for you. Don't you think he's just the sexiest thing you've ever seen? If I weren't so crazy about Rocky, I would have moved in right then."

Charlotte was gazing at Helen expectantly and so was Althea. Helen swallowed, then forced an unsteady laugh. "I'm afraid I don't spend my time ogling the gardeners, Charlotte."

"But, Helen," Althea said with a sly smile, "surely you've noticed him. I have to agree with Charlotte. He's very attractive."

"Do you think so?" Helen asked, and felt sick to her stomach at the evasion. Her eyes frantically searched the terrace for a change of topic. Suddenly she said, "Oh look, there's Babs. I haven't seen her in ages. Doesn't she look good since she's lost weight?"

Althea and Charlotte followed her gaze, taking the bait. A slow smile spread across Charlotte's lips. "Your husband certainly seems to think so, doesn't he, Althea?" the redhead said cattily.

Althea frowned. "She said her husband was working today. I wonder if he knows how she flirts with other men. I've a good mind to tell him."

"What a wonderful idea," Charlotte said, her voice filled with enthusiasm. "Why don't you do it now? There's no sense wasting time." She glanced over her shoulder. "Patty, Mrs. Phillips needs her wrap."

"Must you be so excessively silly, Charlotte?" Althea said in squelching tones.

"Yes, I must," Charlotte replied blithely. "If only to counteract all the stuffiness that seems to be going around lately."

Even Althea's forbidding expression couldn't keep Helen from laughing. Charlotte said all the things Helen wished she could say herself. Suddenly her plump friend spoke again and Helen's laughter turned into a choking cough.

MRS. GALLAGHER AND THE NE'ER-DO-WELL

"Look, Helen, there's your new gardener."

Helen's head jerked up. "Where?"

"Over there. He's talking to Patty." Before Helen could locate him, Charlotte turned to Helen and whispered loudly, "He's coming this way. Introduce me."

As he approached them Tom nodded and murmured, "Mrs. Gallagher," as he passed. Charlotte's nails were digging urgently into Helen's arm. Helen sighed and said tentatively, "Tom?"

He turned back immediately, as though he were attuned to the sound of her voice. "Yes, ma'am?" Could the others see the look in his eyes as he gazed at her?

She swallowed uncomfortably. "Uh . . . what are you doing?"

"The caterer is running low on ice and I've been delegated to fetch more from town."

"But that's not your job," she objected.

He shrugged and smiled. "I don't mind helping out. Patty said everyone pitches in for the garden party."

Charlotte's nails dug deeper, and Helen blinked. "Tom, I'd like you to meet two of my friends, Charlotte Black and Althea Phillips."

"Nice to meet you, Mrs. Black. Mrs. Phillips. Now if you'll excuse me, I'd better get moving before Patty has a fit." He nodded politely then moved through the guests toward the back drive.

Charlotte fanned herself with her napkin. "When he looked at me with those droopy, sexy eyes I almost *died*," she said. "Some people have all the luck. My gardener must be seventy if he's a day."

Helen watched Tom until he disappeared, then she turned to her friends, avoiding their eyes. "I think I'd better start playing hostess," she said weakly. Then without another word she moved away. She could feel Althea's eyes on her as she began to move among her guests.

An hour later Helen left a group of people at poolside and wandered away from the party to a small isolated garden, planted entirely with old-fashioned flowers. The atmosphere at the party was stifling, and she felt the need to get away from the constant talk, talk, talk, if only for a few minutes. Once she had found these affairs stimulating, but everything seemed to have been said years ago. Now she felt she was only living reruns.

Suddenly her arm was caught, and her eyes widened in astonishment as she found herself being swung behind a tall hedge.

"What—" she began, then stopped to look up into Tom's laughing eyes.

He put a finger to his lips and began to pull her toward the orchard. "Come with me, my little petunia," he whispered comically.

She shook her head at his silliness as she tried to remove her arm from his grasp. "Tom, you idiot," she said, laughing. "I can't just leave. I'm the hostess."

"And are therefore entitled to certain privileges," he said. "Who deserves a break more than you?"

"Maybe I deserve one, but I certainly can't take one," she said firmly.

Giving her arm a jerk, he brought her sharply

against his chest. He leaned down to press his lips against hers. The kiss was brief and hard and incredibly sensual.

"Five minutes, Helen," he said against her lips, his voice husky. "You can spare five minutes for this"—his warm mouth found her neck and involuntarily she inclined her head to give him better access—"can't you?"

Helen stared up at him. She couldn't think coherently, not with him so very near. "I'm sorry," she said, her voice breathless. "What did you say?"

He laughed softly, stroked her face, then suddenly they were running. Helen held on to her hat with her free hand, wondering frantically if any minute the heel on one of her shoes would give way. When they reached the orchard, he pulled her abruptly to a halt. Helen leaned against a tree, breathless from laughter and unexpected exercise.

"You're crazy," she said, her voice still unsteady with amusement. "What do you think you're doing?"

"I'm kidnapping you," he said, then he leaned down to pick something up from the grass. "In style," he added, holding two glasses in one hand and a bottle of champagne in the other. "This is the good stuff. The stuff you told Patty to hide from your guests."

"I did no such thing." She took one of the glasses and held it up for him to fill. "I have a feeling you're a born troublemaker," she said regretfully as she took a sip.

Tom studied her for a moment, then tilted her head and bent to kiss drops of champagne from her lips. "That depends on what you call trouble," he murmured.

"Oh, Lord," she said shakily, warily. "You are totally unscrupulous."

He chuckled, sounding pleased with her pronouncement. Pulling her into the crook of his arm, he settled the two of them comfortably against the tree trunk. Together they sank to the ground beneath the flowering fruit tree and sipped champagne. It was a luxurious, sybaritic experience. The minutes sped by unheeded as they laughed and talked like children playing hooky.

"Have you ever really listened to your friends?" he asked lazily. He had moved to lie down with his head in her lap. "This is Texas. They should be saying things like 'y'all' and 'good ol' boy.' Instead, they all talk like Thurston Howell the Third from *Gilligan's Island*."

The comparison made her laugh—a little giddily, thanks to the champagne. Feeling compelled to offer some sort of defense of her friends, she gave him a chastising glance. "You're generalizing. They're not all like that."

His expression was skeptical. "You could have fooled me. I think there must be a school where they all learn to talk with their jaws clenched and jutting forward." He shook his head. "It doesn't matter if it's Rodeo Drive or Park Avenue or Langston, Texas. They all sound alike. I can't understand it. You all have so many rules. You must do this. You mustn't do that. How can you stand it? Don't you ever want to break out of the mold?"

She leaned down, pressing her nose to his. When her eyes crossed, she pulled away and said, "What do you think I'm doing now?"

He chuckled, reaching up to push back a strand of hair that had escaped her smooth, blond chignon. "I think you're getting tipsy."

She shook her head, reaching for the wine bottle. She sighed in regret when no more than a few drops came out. "No, I'm just happy."

"Well, whatever you call it, you're only doing this because I kidnapped you. Don't you ever do anything on your own?"

"Well . . ." She drew out the word slowly, then glanced over her shoulder to make sure they were alone. Leaning closer to him, she whispered, "One time—when I was all alone in the house, I—" She broke off and laughed and began to shake her head.

He sat up, laughing with her. "Come on, tell me. One time when you were alone, you what?"

She motioned for him to come closer and whispered in his ear, "I slid down the banister."

"You devil!" he said, his eyes sparkling with indulgent amusement. "You didn't!"

She nodded emphatically, catching her hat as it slid down onto her forehead. "I did," she said, smiling proudly. She took off the hat and laid it on the grass beside her. "And Patty keeps it so well polished that I couldn't stop and fell right on my—on my—"

"On your ass?" he offered.

"On my posterior," she amended, her voice dignified. Then she giggled and spoiled the image. "I had the most awful bruise for a week or two."

He pulled her into his arms, laughing into her hair. "You're a darling. Do you know that?"

She grinned. "I've often suspected it," she admitted modestly. Reaching up to touch his face, she added, "But it's still nice to hear."

When his face came closer, Helen's eyelids began to drift down. They abruptly opened again when she heard someone whistling very close by. Tom turned with Helen in his arms, and together they watched as Joe approached.

When he drew even with them, the old man nodded, his face blank, and said loudly, "Afternoon, Mrs. Gallagher. Afternoon, Tom."

"Good afternoon, Joe," Helen responded, her voice prim.

"Afternoon, Joe," Tom said, his lips twitching in amusement. "Do you need me to help with something?"

"Naw, I was just on my way to the toolshed." Anger kindled in his pale eyes. "I found aphids on the roses in the back garden."

"No!" Helen said in irreverent horror, causing Tom to shake with silent laughter before he pinched her in chastisement.

"Oh, don't you worry about it, Mrs. Gallagher. No aphid has ever gotten the best of old Joe, and none ever will." He looked beyond them as though envisioning the mass execution of the invaders, then he nodded. "Afternoon, Mrs. Gallagher. Afternoon, Tom."

"Good afternoon, Joe."

"Afternoon, Joe."

As they watched him walk away Tom began to shake with laughter. "He acts like it's the most natural thing in the world to see two people cuddling and drinking champagne under a peach tree."

Helen nodded, holding her hand to her mouth. "I certainly wouldn't want to be an aphid right now. If ever I saw a man with murder in his heart, it's Joe."

From the corner of her eye Helen caught a glimpse of something lavender. But when she looked again, it was gone and she was sure she had imagined it.

Reaching up, Tom tipped her head back. "Now, where were we?" he asked softly.

She smiled. "I believe my lips were just about here." She moved closer. "And if I remember correctly, your hand was here." She brought his hand to her waist, then smiled. "I think the next move is up to you."

He wasn't slow in making it. When his lips touched hers, she felt she had come home after a long, tiring trip. She knew he was special, but she always forgot the way she could lose herself in his arms. When he held her, nothing else seemed important.

Helen felt she could have stayed forever under their tree, but all too soon Tom pulled away and exhaled roughly. "I hate to say it, love, but I think you'd better get back. You were probably missed a long time ago."

She shook her head stubbornly. "I don't want to go back. My garden parties always last forever. As long as the food and drink hold out, no one will notice I'm gone."

"Nevertheless, you've got to get back," he insisted. "You're the hostess. And you can't tell me that Audrey won't notice your absence."

She sighed with regret, admitting the truth of his statement. "I suppose you're right." She stood up and extended her hand. "Walk me home?"

He smiled and rose to his feet. "It'll be my pleasure, Mrs. G."

When they drew close to the terrace, Tom did his best to straighten Helen's hair, but she refused to put the hat on. She slipped back into the milling people, carrying it in her hand. She smiled euphorically at her guests as she passed them, then her eyes widened when she saw Althea Phillips watching her closely.

"Althea!" she called, waving cheerfully. "*Darling, your glass is empty. We've got to correct that immediately*," she said as she walked toward her.

"Hello, Helen," the brunette said. "We've missed you. I hope there was no problem."

Helen caught a strange note in the woman's voice, but she was too happy to wonder about it. "Problem?" she asked, smiling brilliantly. "Who could have problems on a day like this?"

Althea shrugged delicately. "I thought maybe one of your—uh—servants was getting out of hand. Good help is so hard to find."

Helen smiled vaguely. "Really?" She glanced around, seeking more stimulating company. "I'm sure you're right. Oh, there's Charlotte."

Before Helen had taken two steps away, Althea

was whispering to several women nearby, her avid gaze darting occasionally to Helen.

Helen spent the rest of the afternoon going cheerfully from one group to another. It was amazing that she had thought the party dull before. She couldn't remember when she had last laughed so much.

She was to think of that laughter with a twinge of embarrassment later in the evening when the effects of the champagne had worn off. But it was only a twinge, she realized as she sat at the dressing table, brushing her hair. Her overriding emotion was amusement, especially when she imagined what her friends must have thought of her behavior. Had she really thrown her arms around Althea when the other woman was leaving the party? It would probably be all over town the next day that Helen Gallagher was turning into a naughty wino.

She started to lay down the brush, then suddenly she wasn't alone in the mirror. Laughing huskily, she turned around, burying her face in Tom's stomach.

"I thought you'd never get here," she whispered.

"I was helping with the cleanup."

She unbuttoned his shirt and kissed his stomach. "I love your navel."

He laughed huskily. "Of course, you do. It's one of the more attractive navels of the world."

Moving her face against his flesh, she murmured, "I worry about your climbing that trellis. Why don't I just give you a key?"

He smiled a strange smile, his eyes looking

somewhere beyond her as he touched her hair. "And what if someone saw me? What if I got caught in the house?" He lowered his head and captured her eyes. "What then, Mrs. Gallagher?"

She glanced away. What then? she asked herself silently. She cringed when she thought of the embarrassment.

He cupped her chin, raising her face so she would meet his gaze. "Don't worry about it," he said softly. "I accept it. You should too."

"I'm sorry," she whispered, sounding miserable. "You should be very angry with me."

Kneeling beside her, he pulled her into his arms. "How can I be angry with a dream?" he whispered huskily. Rising fluidly, he led her to the bed.

Tom watched Helen as she drifted off to sleep in his arms. She had a right to be exhausted, he thought. She had loved him well. He felt languidly replete. Nothing he had ever experienced could compare to what he found with this lovely woman.

Was it coincidence that had brought him to Langston? he wondered. Or was it something beyond his understanding? Somehow he felt he was meant to find her. Somewhere in her was the key to what he had been searching for. He had to stay until he found the answers.

She was so precious, he thought, studying her beautiful face. It was painful to think of leaving her. Eighteen months ago, in a fanciful moment,

Tom had sworn to go to the ends of the earth to find out what life was all about. Gently he stroked her cheek. Perhaps for him this was the end of the earth.

Seven

When Helen awoke the next morning she felt absolutely wonderful. She spared a moment to pity ordinary people who suffered hangovers when they were indiscreet, and who didn't have dream lovers to make their nights special. Then the rest of the world was callously dismissed, and Tom filled her every thought.

She quickly slipped from the bed, then smiled in a wholly feminine way when she caught sight of her gown lying neatly across a white chair. That was definitely not where she had left it the night before. In fact, she rather thought the last time she had seen it, the silk gown had been hanging drunkenly from the lampshade.

She hugged herself, reveling in the memory. She had to see him again . . . immediately.

Moments later she was running—actually running!—down the stairs on her way to see Tom. She felt like laughing aloud.

She had gained the last step when the front door swung open, and her daughter walked in. Helen hesitated before moving forward cautiously. One look at Audrey's face was enough to tell Helen that her eldest child was absolutely livid. If this were fifteen years earlier, Helen would have prepared herself for a granddaddy of a tantrum.

"Mother," Audrey said, breathing hard between each word, "could I speak with you for a moment?" As Patty walked into the hall she added, "In private."

Helen almost laughed aloud. When her daughter tried to be indignant, the effect was comical. She looked like a chubby little squirrel who had just discovered that her acorns had been stolen.

"Certainly, Audrey," she said, hiding her smile. She followed her daughter into the living room, stopping abruptly when Audrey swung around to face her.

"I can't believe you're laughing," the younger woman said.

"Me?"

Audrey shook her blond head vehemently. "No, don't try to deny it. You're laughing." Suddenly, reluctantly, she smiled. "Okay, I guess I look pretty funny. Actually I just wanted to tell you that I'm not *really* angry that you're having an affair with the gardener."

The blunt words caused Helen to draw in a sharp breath of astonishment. Her laughter disappeared instantly. She closed her eyes, feeling a debilitating feeling spread through her limbs. This was what she had feared from the beginning. She had never consciously thought of what she would do when everyone found out about Tom. But always in the back of her mind was the dread of such a happening.

After a moment she choked out, "How—how did you find out?"

Audrey waved her hand casually. "It was Althea, of course. She's managed to inform everyone over the age of consent in record time—and very gleefully, I might add. No one knows how much is fact and how much is envious imagination." Audrey frowned. "The truth is I may even be a little jealous myself. But why, why in heaven's name did I have to find out through gossip?"

Helen walked to the couch and sat down, feeling her knees give way at the last second. She took a moment to compose her chaotic thoughts and then glanced up. Her smile was tremulous. "Frankly, Audrey, I didn't consider it any of your business." She glanced away and added softly, "I still don't."

"Oh, that's just great," she said, lowering herself awkwardly to the couch beside Helen. "It's the whole town's business. Why should your own daughter be the exception?" She sat silently for a while, then looked at her mother with mischievous curiosity. "How is he?"

For a moment Helen simply stared in confusion. Then when the meaning of the question sunk in, she felt a curious combination of emotions. There was guilt—she couldn't deny that—but overriding the guilt were resentment and anger. And she felt a little sick to her stomach at having her daughter trivialize something that had been so beautiful.

She remained silent for a moment, then said stiffly, "I don't think it's necessary to be crude."

Helen's tone of voice caused Audrey to stare in bewilderment. She seemed to be trying to reach an explanation for something she saw in her mother's eyes, something that caused her concern. Then as though blanking out the only logical conclusion, Audrey shrugged. "Oh, Mother, don't be gauche," Audrey said gently. "This is the twentieth century; everyone knows that women have needs."

"Maybe so," Helen said, her tone dry, her color returning at last. "But somehow it's not the sort of thing I ever expected to be discussing with my own daughter."

"Then your expectations were much too low." Audrey squeezed her mother's hand encouragingly. "A fling is exactly what you need." She grinned broadly. "And Tom is just the man to give it to you."

Helen didn't respond; she couldn't. It took all her effort to lead the conversation to a less harrowing subject. Luckily it wasn't too difficult to convince Audrey to talk about the baby and the plans for its arrival. They spent the rest of her visit examining the clothes Helen had bought for the baby on a recent shopping trip.

Later after Audrey had left, Helen sat quietly in her study. The conversation with her daughter had left a sad feeling in her heart. Seeing the situation through another's eyes had given her a shock she had not expected. If talking about Tom with her daughter—her daughter who loved her—could have such an effect, what would admitting their relationship to the rest of her world do to her?

Closing her eyes, she leaned back in the chair. Everything had been so perfect when she awakened; why did the world have to intrude? For a moment Helen very much resented her own daughter.

How much longer could the fairy tale last? Reality was rapidly approaching, and Helen was so afraid that when it arrived, what she had with Tom would disappear forever. How could she go on with her life if there was no Tom in it?

She had no warning of the lips that were suddenly pressed against hers, but she wasn't slow to respond. Raising her arms, she clung to him feverishly, deepening the kiss, willing him to make her forget everything but his mouth on hers.

Sometime later Helen opened her eyes and found that they were now both occupying the chair and Tom was staring down at her with equal parts of desire, amusement, and curiosity.

He nuzzled her temple. "Remind me to sneak into your study more often," he murmured, gently raising her chin. "What's wrong? You acted like you were drowning and I was the only life raft without holes in it."

She laughed huskily. "That's a little how I felt. It's just that I—" She broke off, unsure of what she wanted to say. "Oh, it was really nothing. Just one of those feelings you get sometimes. Kind of like life has moved to another town without letting you know the new address."

He stroked her face, his dark eyes showing his deep concern. "Oh, love, I'm sorry," he said. "That sounds so lonely."

"Don't," she whispered urgently. "Don't pity me. I would hate that." She smiled. "Everyone feels lonely at times. I'm no different." She looked down at her hands. "Most of the time I'm perfectly satisfied with my life."

He stood and pulled her to her feet. "One of these days we're going to have to talk, Helen. We've been living too close to the edge these past few weeks. Something will have to give sooner or later."

She stared up at him, apprehension filling her eyes. "What do you mean?"

He shook his head. "Not now. You're not ready yet." He brushed his lips across hers. "Besides, my coffee break is over, and I don't want to leave Joe on his own." Reluctantly he removed her hands from his neck and turned to leave.

Suddenly he stopped. "Oh, I forgot. I brought you a present." He pulled something from his shirt pocket and tossed it to her.

Helen caught the small missile in an instinctive movement, then opened her hand. It was a package of M&M's. She felt a lump grow in her throat. "Oh, Lord," she whispered. "Now I'm getting sentimental over a package of candy." She glanced up, a little chuckle escaping her. "Thank you, Tom. I'll treasure them."

He moved to the door. "You're supposed to eat them." He turned back to wink at her. "But save the green ones for tonight."

"For heaven's sake why?"

"Didn't you know?" He lowered his voice. "The green ones make you sexy."

Then he was gone, leaving her laughing. That was his true gift. He always made her laugh. When she looked at Tom, somehow her problems didn't seem so important.

Slowly Helen managed to overcome the empty feeling her talk with Audrey had brought, and for the next few days she pretended nothing had happened. She had never known she was so good at pretending. And she found that after a while the pretense soothed her into believing that there was no problem. She spent her days in ordinary pursuits, anticipating her nights of extraordinary pleasure.

Then almost a week after Audrey's surprise visit, the smooth tenor of Helen's life changed abruptly. Gary arrived home unexpectedly. He had written that he was spending the spring vacation in Florida with friends. So she was surprised when she looked up from her toast one morning to find him striding into the breakfast room.

"Well," she said, laughing as she returned his enthusiastic hug. "So Number One Son has decided to visit the old homeplace. I thought you were in Florida."

"As you can see, I'm not," he said, sitting down and helping himself to a piece of toast. "I decided to come down and bring a little sparkle to the life of my poor gray-haired mother."

"So thoughtful of you, dear," she said. "Now, tell the truth. Did Florida sink under the weight of college freshmen or something?"

MRS. GALLAGHER AND THE NE'ER-DO-WELL

He grinned. "The Dobsons are delayed in New York and won't be there for a couple of days."

"The ugly truth emerges," she said, shaking her head. "So you decided home was better than sleeping on the beach."

He laughed. "Something like that."

While he talked and ate, Helen studied her son. He was looking more like his father every day. But though he tried to act sophisticated, he was still a young boy in many ways. He was excited about being home, but since such a reaction was beneath a college man, he kept up a blasé front.

"I suppose you've dumped all your dirty laundry on our poor unsuspecting Patty?" Helen said as they sat in the living room after breakfast.

Her son grinned, his new sophistication sliding away for a moment. "She didn't mind," he said. "It gave her a chance to grill me. She wanted to make sure I hadn't been corrupted by the decadence in Dallas. She also wanted to stuff ten pounds of food in me to hold me until breakfast."

"I'm sure you objected strenuously," Helen said, smiling.

"You bet. You know, nothing ever changes here," he said, his voice growing thoughtful. "I don't see how you can stand it. I would be bored out of my gourd."

"I don't suppose Langston can compare to the 'decadence in Dallas'?"

He laughed. "Actually I haven't run across that much moral corruption. And I've been looking," he added with a wicked grin. "I've been looking real hard." He jumped up as though the inactivity had suddenly become too much for him. "Gotta go, Mom. I called Mark, and he wants me to meet him in town."

"But you just got here," she protested. "We haven't even talked about your grades yet."

He was already at the door. "We'll talk tomorrow. I promise." As he went out he called back over his shoulder, "By the way, I met the new gardener. He's something." Gary sounded genuinely impressed. "You should talk to him sometime. He's been everywhere and done just about everything you can think of." His young brow creased in thought. "He really knows what it's all about." Then he walked out, leaving Helen in thoughtful silence.

Tom leaned over the lawn mower beside the toolshed, tightening a bolt that had nothing to do with the mechanical trouble he was looking for. He had stripped off his shirt earlier and perspiration was running down his back.

It was difficult for him to keep his mind on the broken piece of machinery before him. More and more often a vision of a bewitchingly lovely face shattered his concentration. He smiled. All thoughts led to Helen.

Suddenly he glanced up, and she was standing beside him. "What a coincidence," he said, rocking back on his heels. "I was just thinking about you. Of course, you could come at any time of the day and the same would be true."

MRS. GALLAGHER AND THE NE'ER-DO-WELL

She laughed softly, brushing her hair back. "What are you doing? It looks complicated."

"I'm trying to fix this." He indicated the lawn mower. "But I think it's gilflirted."

"Gilflirted?"

He laughed at her expression. "That's what Joe says. I tried to look it up last night, but I couldn't find it. I think it means busted."

When she fell silent, Tom returned to his work. He could feel her watching him, but made no comment. In a lot of ways Helen was less inhibited now than when he had first met her. But there were still times that she withdrew to a place that Tom couldn't reach.

He worried during those times. He even felt lonely. But he never pressed. She would tell him what was on her mind when she was ready.

After a moment she said, "You certainly made an impression on Gary."

He grinned, wiping his hands on a rag that smelled strongly of gasoline. "He made one on me too. I like him, Helen. He seems like a nice kid."

"I think—I think he likes you too."

Something was definitely up, he thought. Her strange tone of voice brought him to his feet. He examined her face for a clue to what was going on in her mind. "Why do you say it like that?" he asked finally. "Did you think he wouldn't?"

Helen frowned, her brow creasing in thought. How could she answer that? she wondered. "I guess I didn't think of it at all," she said helplessly.

He stared at her in silence for a moment, and then a grim smile twisted his lips. "The ultimate insult," he murmured. Abruptly he turned and walked away from her.

Hours later Helen was sitting alone in the study. She couldn't get over the look in Tom's eyes when she had last seen him. Without intending to, she had hurt him. How could she have been so careless? She had to find a way to make it up to him.

She glanced out the window. It was odd how gray everything looked when he wasn't with her. How could one person affect her life so completely?

Suddenly the front door slammed with extreme force. Standing quickly, she walked out of the study, then stopped abruptly. Gary stood in the hall, his face contorted with some violent emotion. Helen felt the color drain from her face. She knew what was coming, and she didn't know if she could survive another confrontation with one of her children.

"How could you!" he rasped out. Without giving her a chance to respond, he raked a trembling hand through his already disheveled hair. "Do you realize that the whole town is talking about my mother and—and a *bum*?" He swung around to face her. "What in hell are you doing? Do you think you're Lady Chatterley or something?"

Helen remained silent. Words seemed inadequate. She wanted so badly to comfort him, but she couldn't allow her son to push her into defending herself. She refused to behave like a thief caught in the act.

"You're making a damn fool of yourself," he continued, his voice unsteady with emotion. "Half the town thinks he's after your money. The other half thinks you're only after his body." Suddenly his fist crashed into the wall. "Damn! My own mother, screwing the *gardener*!"

She slapped him. She had never slapped Gary before, but she slapped him now. And she slapped him hard. He backed away from her, his eyes astonished, as though he were watching a goldfish turn into a shark.

She glanced down at the hand that had struck him, staring at it as though it belonged to someone else. Inhaling shakily, she said, "You're . . . you're angry and hurt. I realize that. But I have never allowed you to speak to me like that, and I won't start now. If you want to talk about this like adults, that's fine; we can do that."

Please, she begged silently, *please give me the strength to get through this*. She raised a trembling hand, an unconscious gesture of entreaty. But Gary stared at it as though it were something foreign, something dreadful.

She dropped her hand, feeling all emotion drain out of her. "But if you continue to act like a child," she said stiffly, "then you'll be treated as one."

Helen closed her eyes in defeat when the door slammed behind him. Opening them slowly, she stared for a long time at the front door. Slowly, wearily she turned and walked back into the study.

Everything was falling apart, she thought in confusion. She was no longer in control of her life, and she didn't know what to do about it. Her head ached and her body echoed the throbbing pain.

Although she stayed awake for hours, waiting,

Helen was almost glad when Tom didn't climb the trellis that night. She needed time to think, time to find some answers.

Staring up at the dark ceiling, she replayed the scene with Gary in her mind. Suddenly she laughed brokenly. "Lady Chatterley?" she whispered in the darkness. Was that what he was studying in college?

She rolled over restlessly. What should she do? Gary would calm down eventually, maybe even enough to be reasonable. But Helen had the feeling that the trouble with her son was only the beginning. She had taken her relationship with Tom for granted; after the first time they had made love, she had not thought of the end of their affair. In fact, she had assiduously avoided thinking about that.

She sighed heavily. She supposed that she would have to think about it now. Tom wouldn't stay forever. Joe's nephew Howie would be able to return to work any day, leaving Tom without a job. And where did that leave Helen? How on earth was she going to go on without him? she wondered in despair.

These thoughts and more plagued her until she fell into a restless sleep. It was barely dawn when she slipped out of the house and wandered out toward the orchard. A thin mist was clinging to the grass as she walked slowly, unaware of the dampness penetrating her clothing.

She smiled, remembering the day they had sat together under the flowering peach tree. She had acted silly that day, and it wasn't entirely the fault of the wine. With Tom beside her, she felt free to be silly, or sad, or angry. He accepted all these things as a part of her.

Would he accept her carelessness too? she wondered wistfully. Then she looked up and Tom was standing directly in front of her.

He smiled wryly. "Life is certainly complicated, isn't it, Snow Queen?"

She laughed shakily. "It certainly is."

He leaned against a tree, glancing down at the blades of grass he held in his hand. "I missed you last night."

She closed her eyes and nodded, knowing he couldn't have missed her as much as she had missed him. It was a physical impossibility.

"Helen, I'm sorry I acted like an idiot yesterday," he said softly. "It was stupid."

"No, it wasn't. You were right. It was an insult." She opened her eyes to gaze at him earnestly. "But I didn't mean it that way. I simply didn't stop to think."

He inhaled and pulled her into his arms. "I know. I should have been more understanding." He tilted her head up. "Smile for me, Helen."

When she tried to obey him, her lips trembled. She dipped her head to hide her face in his shoulder, clinging to him tightly.

He lifted her chin, staring into her eyes in concern. "Something else is wrong, isn't it?"

"Everything," she said, laughing shakily.

"Come on." He put his arm around her waist and urged her forward. "Come back to the Winnebago with me and tell me about it."

Five minutes later she was seated across the

table from him with her fingers wrapped around a coffee cup. Miraculously things didn't look so grim from this vantage point.

"It's all a tempest in a teapot," she said after explaining to him what had happened with her son the day before. "Audrey thinks it's great that I'm having a 'fling'—Lord, I hate that word—and Gary acts like I've just sold military secrets to the Russians."

He watched her carefully. "How do you feel about their knowing?"

She stared at the ceiling for a moment. "It's strange, but my first reaction was anger that the world—in the form of my children—had intruded on our relationship." She grimaced. "Then, like the true coward I am, I was embarrassed that everyone was talking about me."

"Everyone?" he said skeptically.

"You know what I mean." She shook her head wryly. "It's all so sad. Funny and sad. I've always felt sorry for women who make fools of themselves over men. Now I'm as big a fool as any of them."

He stood up, turning away as he poured another cup of coffee. His voice was casual when he asked, "You honestly feel you've made a fool of yourself?"

She winced. His voice was *too* casual. Moving to stand behind him, she touched his arm, gently turning him to face her. "Not because we made love," she said softly. "Please believe that."

He stared deeply into her eyes as though he were trying to look inside her soul. After a moment he nodded. "I believe you."

She moved to sit on the couch. Leaning her head

back, she sighed heavily. "I know I shouldn't mind so much. It's just that I hate the thought of careless people gossiping and laughing about my personal life."

"I think it's time we talked," he said, going to the couch to sit beside her. He picked up her hand and stared at it for a moment. Then, glancing up, he said, "I think the problem is the restricted life you lead. You can't see beyond your self-imposed boundaries. Langston is only a town, Helen. It's exactly like a thousand other towns. Maybe the surface is different, but underneath it's the same. Ten to one someone in Langston is sleeping with someone else's wife; and someone hates his boss and the IRS and all homosexuals; and someone else secretly wears his girlfriend's underwear under his suit. It's not all that different. But if you think it's the world, you're wrong."

She smiled, thinking of local citizens who fit his description to a T. "But I have to deal with Langston," she said earnestly. "It's *my* world."

"It doesn't have to be." He held both of her hands tightly as though to give her some of his strength. "You've asked me several times about my life and why I live it the way I do. I'd like to tell you about it now. Will you listen?"

She stared at him for a moment. What he was going to say was obviously important to him. She hesitated without really knowing why; then she nodded. "Of course, I'll listen."

"If you had seen me three years ago, you probably wouldn't have recognized me. Physically I wasn't all that different, but what's inside always shows on the outside. And three years ago . . . well, to tell the truth three years ago I was emotionally drained. I gave everything—love, devotion, loyalty—to my work. I owned one of the most successful small public relations firms on the East Coast."

He smiled. "Some people would say I had everything. And I was still on my way up. Nothing could stop me. *No one* could stop me. Not even my wife." When he caught her questioning glance, he shrugged. "I married late and divorced early. She couldn't compete with the business. It didn't bother me. It was annoying, sure. But it wasn't really *important*." He held her hands tighter. "That sounds terrible, but I'm trying to give you a true picture of the way things were."

"I understand," she said quietly, hating the self-disgust she heard in his voice.

"Then two years ago something happened. It wasn't anything out of the ordinary for the business world. A business opponent had played some dirty tricks. My people were slow to catch on, and by the time I found out, my company was on the rocks." He inhaled. "I knew the rules of the game, so I did the only thing I could. I set out to destroy him. In the process I ruined my health. The pressure brought on some kind of attack. It was like my body was rebelling against misuse. Too much pressure and alcohol. Too many cigarettes and late nights. All the things that went with my kind of life. I was hospitalized—against my will, I might add. My doctor said it was only a warning, but if I kept up the pace I had set for myself, the next time would be much more serious."

Tom was completely lost in the past now. He stared out the window at the horizon as though his life were being played there.

"For the first time in years I had empty hours to fill. Hours that I spent thinking. Maybe it was a realization of my own mortality that struck me; I don't know. Whatever it was, I took a good look at myself. Asked some questions. What was I fighting for? Money? Success? I had both, but what did I really have? Money is nothing. Success is something so nebulous that no one can even define it. I looked around and found a hundred men exactly like me. We were like dogs chasing our own tails and not going anywhere."

Suddenly he smiled. "I hate to say it, but that was as far as I got in my inner search. I don't know what I would have done if one of the nurses hadn't brought me a copy of Thoreau's *Walden*. I started reading it to get away from my thoughts, and suddenly I couldn't put it down. It was as though he had written the book just for me. Suddenly I knew what was missing. Life, the real stuff, the deep-down guts of it, was missing. I was only playing around on the edges." He shook his head. "I wasn't looking for some kind of Utopia where nothing ever goes wrong. But like Thoreau, I wanted to capture life and examine it. And if it was mean, then I wanted to experience 'the whole and genuine meanness of it.' And if it was good, then I wanted that too. I simply wanted to find out what life was like, who I truly was."

He shifted. "When they released me from the hospital, I started putting the business back on its feet." He grinned. "I'm afraid my pride wouldn't let me walk away a loser. Then I turned the whole thing over to my assistant. I sold him the whole works. He deposited the money in my bank in New York—I'm not even sure how much I have—and then I left." He shrugged. "About a year ago I set out to see America. I started on the West Coast because that was as far away from the past as I could get. I started working my way across. Not because I had to, but because it seemed to me to be the only way to get to know people rather than just observe them."

He put his arm around her and pulled her closer. "Helen, you wouldn't believe the people I've met—in Oregon and Utah and Nebraska. Wonderful people. People who know what life's really about. They've given me so much."

He gazed deeply into her eyes. "There was only one thing missing. You, Helen. You should have been there with me. I had no one to turn to and say, 'Isn't that strange?' or 'Isn't that wonderful?' I didn't have you to share it with." He captured her chin, his grip firm. "I want you to marry me and come with me."

Eight

Helen was speechless. She simply sat there and stared at Tom. Twice she opened her mouth to speak, then closed it helplessly when no sound came forth.

He laughed shortly. "You look like I just told you your dog died." He clasped her face between his hands. "Helen, love," he said, his voice intense, his dark eyes shining with emotion. "I know I've taken you by surprise, but haven't you thought about it at all?" He shook his head in a self-mocking gesture. "I haven't been able to think of anything else. I know it will mean a big change for you. But I promise you won't be deprived of anything important. And there's no way I can leave without you now."

He examined her face, taking in the confusion, then he gripped her hands tightly and asked, "Could you let me leave?"

She caught her breath at the question. Could

she do without him? What would it be like never to have him appear beside her and brighten the world? Never to feel his arms around her just when she needed him most? Could she let him go?

"No," she whispered, shaking her head wildly. "No, I don't think I could."

"Then marry me," he urged gently. "Come with me to see the world. Share it with me."

She ran her fingers through her hair in confusion. "Everything is happening so fast. You've given me so much to think about." She waved one slender hand weakly. "Your life. Your values."

She closed her eyes for a moment, remembering everything, all the grotesquely pompous things she had said to him and thought of him. The enormity of her mistake caused her lips to twist in self-reproach.

"And I criticized you for not doing something worthwhile," she whispered in disbelief. "You gave up everything that most people consider important. All for your principles." She inhaled shakily. "I've never met anyone with that kind of strength. To tell you the truth I'm a little awed." She glanced at him quickly, then away again. "I can't tell you how much I admire you."

He leaned his head back against the wall, his eyelids dropping down over his deep brown eyes as though he were suddenly weary. After a moment he said slowly, "Admiration?" As though the word were sour, he frowned and shook his head. "Admiration is a good thing. A good thing to feel for your Sunday school teacher or the President, but"—he pinned her with his gaze—"is that all? Is that all you feel for me?"

"No—no, of course not," she whispered. "I—I care very much for you."

One corner of his mouth curved up in an almost wistful expression. "That's a start. Now answer another question. Could you go on with your life as though this hadn't happened between us?" He gently stroked her cheek. "Aren't you 'half-sick of shadows,' Helen?"

"Shadows?" she asked. Then when she understood his meaning she laughed huskily. "The Lady of Shalott?" She shrugged and said with wry humor, "I guess I prefer her to Lady Chatterley."

"Gary?" he asked, his expression sympathetic.

She nodded, gazing at Tom in silence. Would she ever understand him? He was really something. With all that was happening between them, he could still be concerned with her problems.

"I'm sorry," he said gently. He leaned down to kiss her—a healing kiss, a kiss to give her sustenance. "I know that was painful for you, but believe me, love, it's a perfectly normal reaction. His protective instincts are coming out. He'll probably feel differently when he finds out we're going to be married."

She inhaled sharply. Married. How could she expect Gary to accept it? Marriage was something she was having difficulty accepting herself. "I don't know about that. Gary and Audrey have both come to expect a certain kind of behavior from me," she admitted hesitantly. "Anything new is bound to throw them off."

"But they're adults. Surely they know you have your own life to live." He shook his head, laughing in wry amusement. "This reminds me of an old joke. A man saw a woman carrying a boy about seven years old. When he asked her if the boy was her son, she said yes, her face full of love as she looked down at the child. The man didn't want to be rude, but finally his curiosity got the better of him and he said, 'Can't he walk?' To which the woman responded, 'Yes, but thank heaven he doesn't have to.'"

Helen laughed. "You're exaggerating, I know. But I'm afraid it's the nature of children, even grown children like mine, to be selfish. I know they love me and want what's best for me. The only problem is, it's always their idea of what's best."

"You don't think they'll approve of me?" he asked, studying her carefully.

"I may be an indulgent mother, but I wouldn't ask them whether they approved of you," she said, shaking her head emphatically. "That's not important."

"No," he agreed quietly. "The important thing is whether or not *you* approve of me."

Helen knew he needed something from her. Not just her approval, but something more, something deeper. And it was something she was afraid she couldn't give him right now. Maybe she would never be able to. He wanted her to give him everything that was inside her. All the emotions she had locked away. All the feelings that were buried so deep that exposure would bring pain.

She didn't enjoy having to admit to herself that

she didn't know how much there was in her to give. He was so dreadfully open with her. How could she match that? She had never felt so inadequate in all her life.

She inhaled, staring down at her hands for a moment. She would simply have to give him what she could. "When we first met," she said softly, "I said a lot of stupid things. You tried to shatter my defenses from the very beginning." She smiled poignantly. "What you didn't know was that you were succeeding like crazy. To combat my own vulnerability, I tried to make you believe—I tried to make myself believe—that you were beneath me."

Glancing up, she met his eyes directly. "I've always known that you are something special. So special that I feel . . . less." She shook her head helplessly, unable to find the right words. "I feel useless and silly in comparison. It's almost like comparing an anecdote with the truth."

He exhaled shakily then placed his hands on either side of her face. "Don't you know?" he said hoarsely. "Don't you know that without you there is no truth in me? You're the key to everything."

Although Helen felt she didn't deserve it, she accepted his statement, just as she accepted his lips. And she recognized the deep emotion behind both. It was quite a while before they got back to the question of her children.

"I want so badly to say yes. But I just don't know, Tom," Helen said, shaking her head as she rested against him. "You're asking me to drop everything—my whole life—and leave Langston, leave my children." She glanced up hesitantly. "Why couldn't we stay here?"

He frowned, leaning back to think about her question. Deep grooves of concentration formed in his forehead, his eyes narrowing. He studied her with unnerving intensity.

After a moment he raised one hand, palm up in a helpless gesture. "This is hard for me to explain, Helen." He smiled wryly. "The truth is I'm scared." He stared down at her, his eyes caressing her face. "If we stayed, could you ever be completely free of the past? You're changing in a wonderful way. The you that has always been hidden inside is out in the open for the first time." He leaned his head back in a tired gesture. "But if we stayed in Langston, would you gradually incorporate me into your life and slide back into old patterns? And is it selfish of me to want to be the most important thing in your life?"

He shook his head. "You tell me, Helen. Should we stay?" He smiled. "Don't look so scared. I trust you." He touched her lips with his thumb, then kissed her as though giving her his complete trust.

Helen felt the enormity of the gesture weigh on her mind, her heart. She tried to imagine what their relationship would be like if they stayed. Would she be lessening what was between them?

"No, you're right. If we marry, we'll have to leave. At least for a while," Helen said at last. "I have to think it over. There are so many things to consider. Can you give me some time?"

Although he felt disappointment surge through him, Tom knew what it had cost her to get to this point. He wouldn't press her. She was about to make the most important decision of her life.

Please, God, he begged silently. Let her make the right one. Getting a grip on his emotions, he smiled down at her. "Of course. We'll talk again tomorrow."

She sagged in relief, smiling her gratitude. "Thank you," she whispered. "And thank you for being so understanding about everything. I know I've been a pain. . . ." She paused. When he didn't deny it, she laughed reluctantly. "How ungallant of you. Well, I suppose I deserve it. But wasn't it your Thoreau who said to beware all enterprises that require new clothes?" She smiled. "I haven't got a thing to wear in a Winnebago."

Throwing back his head, he laughed and pulled her close. "There are a lot of things to work out," he said. He reached up to stroke her cheek gently. "But we can do anything as long as we're together. Believe that." He inhaled and moved away from her. "What will you do now?"

She ran her fingers through her already disheveled hair and shook her head. "I don't know. I've got to think. I'll probably go hibernate in the study and try to think everything through logically."

Tom wanted to tell her to use her heart, not logic, but he didn't. She had to work it out in her own way. "Will you have dinner with me tonight?"

"Yes—oh, wait." She moaned. "I forgot. I'm supposed to have dinner tonight with the Phillipses—Althea and her husband—and Charlotte and Rocky."

"Rocky?" he asked, eyeing her in disbelief. "No one is named Rocky."

She laughed. "Yes, well, don't tell him that. It's awful, I know, but much to my amazement, I find I like him. I'm meeting them all at the country club."

He watched her closely as he said, "I could always come with you."

For a moment she looked confused, then suddenly her eyes opened wide as the idea took root. "Tom," she said urgently, "that's it. Yes, you'll come with me."

He was shocked. "Are you sure? I was just teasing you." He frowned. "I think maybe you'd better think this over. You could be letting yourself in for a lot of static."

She shook her head vigorously. "It doesn't matter. Everyone already knows about us. I simply can't face another meaningless social evening. Come with me and save me from boredom."

His eyes were worried, but he couldn't resist her appeal. "Sure. If that's what you want."

She stood up, then leaned down to kiss his cheek. "It's what I want."

Helen could feel him watching her as she walked toward the house, but she didn't look back. She needed to keep a cool head to think things through. Looking around the yard, she was amazed to find that it was still very early. So much had happened. It felt like hours since she had awakened that morning.

And if she thought the morning was long, the rest of the day seemed to roll by on square wheels. Her brain refused to work. She tried again and again to sort through the complications of her situation, but all she could think of was the fact that Tom loved her and wanted to marry her.

She tried to imagine how her children would take the news, but found it impossible to anticipate their reactions. Since Gary had not come home the night before, Helen couldn't even ask him a few pointed questions about how he would feel about her remarrying.

She was worried about Gary. It wasn't like him to stay out all night. But Helen felt she would only make things worse if she tried to find him. Her son had friends in Langston who would take him in.

She shook her head, wondering briefly what people would think about his behavior. Then even the thought of gossip diminished in importance as she lost herself in imagining a life with Tom.

Tom stepped out of the Winnebago, feeling a little uncomfortable in the gray suit he was wearing. It had been a while since he had worn anything other than jeans, he realized. He stared for a moment at the house, wondering what she was thinking. Would she back out? Somehow he had the idea that if she had had time to think, she wouldn't have offered the invitation.

Taking a deep breath, he turned and walked toward the back garden. He wasn't surprised to find Joe still working. The old man was hunkered down on his knees turning over the dirt in a bed of dainty star-shaped flowers. His rough, lined hands looked too big and awkward to handle such delicate plants, but it seemed as though the plants understood him and allowed the intrusion.

Joe looked up as Tom bent down to help him. "I thought you were through for the day."

"You're not," Tom replied quietly.

"That's because these plants are my kids," he said gruffly. "You don't leave your family when you get off work. You now, you're young. You oughta be out getting together a real family." Without looking up, he added, "Besides, you're going to get those fancy clothes dirty."

Tom glanced at the suit, then stood, dusting his hands off on a white handkerchief. "Yeah, I guess you're right. Have you ever had a real family, Joe?"

The old man remained silent for a long time. "Onced. My wife died, and they took the baby away from me 'cause they said I couldn't take care of it." He didn't look up, but continued with his work. "It was a long time ago. Everything heals. I have my plants now. That's all I need."

There wasn't any pain in Joe's voice. It was curiously objective, as though he were talking about someone else. And that made the stark words worse. An emotional harangue against life wouldn't have affected Tom nearly as deeply.

Tom watched Joe work in silence, the stillness of the evening acting as a tranquilizer. When he had finished the bed, Joe stood and squinted as he gazed at Tom.

"Howie's due back any day now."

Tom nodded. "Yes, I know. I guess you'll be glad to have him."

MRS. GALLAGHER AND THE NE'ER-DO-WELL

Joe shrugged. "He's all right. He's big enough to do the hard work and dumb enough to not mind. What about you? What'll you do now?"

Tom glanced up at the sky. The stars were beginning to come out, their light merging with the last of the sun. "I've got . . . plans," he said. "But I won't know until tomorrow if they're going to work out."

Joe made no comment immediately. He bent down to pick up his tools, then as he started to walk away, he glanced back over his shoulder. "She's a good woman. A strong woman," he said quietly. "Just give her time to find that out." Then he walked off into the dark.

Tom began to turn, then stopped abruptly. Helen was standing on the path, staring at him.

"You look . . . wonderful," she said hesitantly. She had never seen Tom in a suit, and for a moment she was almost intimidated. He seemed a sophisticated, sensual stranger. Then he smiled and imperceptibly she relaxed. He was still Tom.

"You're not exactly chopped liver yourself," he said. "It makes me wish we were going out alone for a romantic dinner instead of meeting your friends."

She agreed with him, and on the drive to the country club, she felt the nervous anticipation building inside her. By the time they walked into the dining room, Helen was prepared for disaster.

It seemed as though everyone in the dining room were watching them. The country-club dining room had long been a favorite of Helen's. The understated elegance of the cool blue room had always had a soothing effect on her. But not tonight. As she glanced around she saw so many acquaintances, so many friends. They were dressed as they usually dressed; their faces held familiar expressions. But in some indefinable way tonight everything seemed different. Helen was isolated from them. She was odd man out.

When Tom spotted Althea across the room, he took Helen's arm, giving it a bracing squeeze. Leaning down, he whispered, "Shall we go beard the lion in her very elegant lair?"

She drew in a deep breath, raised her chin, and nodded firmly.

Charlotte was sitting beside Althea, and she was the first to notice them. She grinned openly, punching Rocky with her elbow. He glanced up and, apparently noticing nothing out of the ordinary, waved to Helen. That brought them to Althea's attention.

The older woman jerked her head around, her movements as sharp as the lines of her face. Her eyes widened, first in shock, then with a kind of malicious enjoyment.

"Helen, *darling*," she said enthusiastically as she greeted them. "It's so nice to see you. You've been so busy lately. I really miss our little luncheons." She looked up at Tom as though she had just noticed his presence. "And who is— Oh, wait. I believe we've already met."

Tom nodded, smiling. "Yes, we met the day of the garden party, Mrs. Phillips."

"Yes, of course." She glanced at her husband. "I don't believe you've met my husband, Ronald." Her husband extended his hand, his smile polite. "Ronald," Althea continued, "this is Tom Peters . . . Helen's gardener."

If the atmosphere had not been so tense, Ronald's expression would have been comical. He withdrew his hand hastily as though he were afraid Tom would steal it right off his arm. He glanced nervously around the room, either to convince himself he was actually there or to check which of his friends had noticed he was having dinner with a gardener.

Conversation at dinner was sluggish, to say the least. But eventually Ronald, with Althea's encouragement, decided to show Tom that he had no hope of keeping up with the topics common in circles of the elite.

When Tom showed that he was conversant with most aspects of music, travel, and business, the Phillipses began to look more and more grim, while Charlotte seemed to be having the time of her life. Rocky nodded occasionally and attended to his dinner.

Somehow Helen managed to behave naturally, smiling and nodding, occasionally inserting a pertinent few words. She was proud of Tom, but by the time dessert arrived, her smile was becoming a little strained.

Having failed to get the better of Tom, the Phillipses decided to monopolize the conversation completely. Both tall, dark, and thin, they looked depressingly similar. Althea would make a statement and Ronald would either vehemently back it up or hesitantly add to it. They spent exactly fifteen minutes discussing Ronald junior and his brilliant career at business college. Then seven and a half minutes were devoted to politics. From there the conversation dwindled to a discussion of what was happening with the "right" people in Langston.

"I see Gary is home from college," Althea said sweetly, bringing Helen's attention back to those at the table.

Helen nodded. "For a few days," she murmured. "He has plans to visit friends in Florida when he leaves here."

"How nice. You must adore having him back. I know how much we're enjoying Ronald junior." She paused. "You know, Helen darling, I really hate having to mention it"—Althea's expression was anything but regretful—"but I can't stand people who are continually minding everyone else's business."

She paused expectantly, then frowned when Ronald was the only one to agree that such people were a nuisance. When no further encouragement was forthcoming, she continued. "But there are some things one simply can't keep quiet about." Her smile was condescending. "I've always felt that we mothers should stick together."

"Oh, for heaven's sake," Charlotte said, laying down her fork in exasperation. "You have everyone's undivided attention, Althea. Spit it out."

Althea ignored the redhead with obvious contempt. "The fact is, dear, Ronald junior tells me that Gary has been drinking rather heavily lately." Suddenly her small eyes widened in assumed horror. "Oh, Helen, you don't suppose . . . ? No, of course not."

When Helen felt Tom tense beside her, she quickly laid her hand on his arm. This was something she had to handle herself. "Get on with it, Althea," Helen said grimly, knowing very well what was coming next.

"Well," the other woman said, leaning across the table to whisper. "You don't suppose Gary could have found out about your *liaison*, do you?"

The silence at the table was deafening. Helen felt angry heat rise to her face. She inhaled slowly, then pushed back her chair to stand up. "Althea," she said tightly, "what my son and I do are none of your business. And frankly, *darling*, in my opinion you have about as much charm and tact as a Roller Derby queen."

There was a moment of stunned silence, then Charlotte and Rocky began howling with laughter, the redhead raising one fist in a gesture of victory. Tom's expression was unreadable, but not his eyes; they were shining with love and pride.

Helen smiled slightly as she picked up her purse. "Now if you'll all excuse us, we're going home."

Rocky glanced at Charlotte, who nodded, and the two of them stood also. "Yeah," Rocky said. "We've gotta go too. I just remembered something important we have to do."

The four of them walked out together. When they reached the parking lot, Charlotte turned to Rocky. "What do we have to do that's so important?"

He grinned boyishly. "They're showing three

hours of *The Brady Bunch* reruns on Channel Three."

Helen faced them, her eyes filled with gratitude. "I want to thank you both." She grimaced as she felt the inadequacy of the words. "What you did just now means a lot to me. More than you'll ever know."

Tom nodded. "And I'll add my thanks to that. I'm glad to know Helen has friends like you two."

Rocky shrugged casually. "I didn't want to finish dessert anyway." He glanced back at the club. "Somebody should tell the cook that the cherries have turned on him."

Charlotte rolled her eyes at Helen, then hugged her tightly. "Don't worry about what that bony bitch says, Helen," Charlotte whispered.

"I'm not," Helen said. "But I am worried about my behavior. I know Althea has problems. I've always known it and I should have been more tolerant."

Then Charlotte said something that shocked Helen. "Her only problem is the size of her brain," she said in disgust. "Anyone with any kind of mind at all could see that you're happier than you've been in years. Hold on to it," she said urgently. She glanced at Tom, then at Rocky. "Believe me, I intend to."

When Charlotte rejoined her escort, he put his arm around her, guiding her toward his sports car. Before they faded from sight, Helen heard her auburn-haired friend say, "Rocky, honey, the cherries had a brandy sauce on them."

"You mean somebody did that on purpose?" he asked, shaking his head in disbelief.

Tom and Helen laughed, partly in genuine amusement, partly in relief that the evening was finally over. For Helen, Althea's heckling was forgotten the instant she thought of what was ahead of her. She still had a decision to make.

By mutual agreement they separated for the evening after Helen had parked the car. When he kissed her good night, Tom conveyed the urgency he felt. They both knew how important the next twelve hours were to their future. He caught her hand as she climbed from the car.

"Helen," he whispered. "Think fast . . . please."

Later when she crawled into bed, she smiled wistfully, remembering the words, the tone of his voice, the look in his eyes. She lay in the dark, going over every word he had said earlier in the day, thinking about what leaving with him would mean to her life.

"I love him," she whispered to the empty room. It was the first time she had admitted it to herself. She loved him and she desperately wanted to spend the rest of her life with him. Why couldn't she just say yes?

Everything was so confusing—everything that should have been simple. People who loved each other should be together, Helen thought. But why did it have to be so frightening?

She rolled onto her side, knowing that sleep wouldn't come easily tonight. She wanted to be with Tom. Oh, Lord, she wanted him badly. But Helen also knew that once he touched her, she wouldn't be able to think objectively about anything. And she simply had to think. She had to work out what the change would mean for her. She owed it to herself and to him to be sure of the next step.

She closed her eyes. How could she simply leave everything—everything that made her life stable—behind? He said she had to live her own life, but that wasn't what he meant. He wanted her to live *his* life. A way of life alien to her. Could she do it?

Across the vast expanse of lawn Tom was also lying awake. He pulled his hands from behind his head and raised himself up to lean against the wall of the camper. As he moved, the sheet slid down, exposing his hard, lean, tanned hips. He stared broodingly out the window at the stars, wondering what she was thinking of now. Wondering if she was thinking of him. Wondering if she had yet discovered how she felt about him.

He had tossed and turned on the bed for hours, asking himself the same question. Did Helen love him enough to come with him?

Eighteen months ago he had left everything behind with the grand purpose of finding out what life was all about. In the night sky he could see worlds upon worlds, worlds stretching into infinity. There were so many more things he wanted to explore. But he forgot everything when he looked into Helen's eyes.

He had placed his life in her hands. Did she know that? he wondered. How would he be strong enough to leave if she said no? But how could he stay and continue to be her illicit lover? He shifted restlessly. Could he spend the rest of his life climbing the trellis to her bedroom?

A muted sound pulled his eyes away from the window and suddenly she was there, standing beside the bed. He closed his eyes as a strange weakness overcame him, then without a word, he pulled her down to lie beside him.

His hand shook as he stroked her. He leaned down, smoothing his lips over her shoulders, her neck. Everything—life, love, peace—everything was in his arms.

"I was afraid you would say no," he whispered huskily.

She touched his face, and his hair, and his chest. She couldn't get enough of him. "I almost did," she admitted sadly. "I thought about how I would be leaving everything behind: my family, my home, my friends." Framing his face with her hands, she stared deep into his eyes. "Then suddenly it came to me. *You* are my everything. If you leave without me, I'll have very little left . . . among many shadows."

He hugged her close, overwhelming emotion robbing him of words. He hadn't realized how afraid he had been. Not until relief made him weak. "I love you, Helen," he whispered at last.

Her hand trembled against his face. They were only three words, but they meant everything to her. "And I love you," she said huskily. "More than you know. More than I knew."

Neither of them could wait any longer. It had

been too long since they had loved. They came together silently, urgently.

Some time later, after many whispered words of love, Helen glanced up at Tom hesitantly. "We still need to talk," she said softly. "I want to go with you. I *have* to go with you. But I don't want to disappoint you."

"You could never do that."

She laughed wryly. "Don't be too sure. I'm trying to be honest with myself and with you. You've seen the kind of life I live. I don't know how good I'll be at your kind of life." She paused, then said slowly, "Could we try it your way for a couple of months? Then if either of us is dissatisfied we can try to find some way to work it out . . . together," she hastened to assure him. "Always together."

Tom understood her hesitation. He was asking a lot of her. That she was even willing to try said something for her courage. He tipped up her chin. "All I ever wanted was a chance, Helen. I'm not asking you to make any final moves—other than marrying me. We can work out any problems that come up. We'll do it however you want."

Nine

Helen came awake slowly, smiling when she felt lips on her breasts. Wrapping her arms around Tom, she hugged him, moving against him dreamily as a small sound of satisfaction escaped her.

"Good morning, Mrs. Gallagher," he said, his mouth warm against her skin.

"Yes," she said happily. "It is a good morning. In fact, it's an excellent morning."

He grinned. "I hope you still think so when you leave here, my love. What are you going to do when Patty catches you sneaking into the house?"

"I shall order coffee," she said, waving her hand airily. She lifted her arms to stretch in a deliciously sinful movement, then doubled up with a squeal of laughter when Tom began to nibble on her stomach.

"There's no point in continuing the charade," she continued, excitement filling her pale blue eyes. "As soon as I get everything organized, we'll blow this joint . . . together. Together," she repeated softly. "Do you know how wonderful that sounds to me? To know that every morning when I wake up I'll find you beside me?"

He rested his chin in his hand to stare down at her. "You realize what that means, don't you?" he said, his voice mock-serious. She stared at him for a moment, then shook her head. "It means you have to spend every night with me too," he said fiendishly.

She put her hand to her forehead in a graceful swoon. "Oh, no," she said. "You didn't tell me that."

His lip quivered in amusement. "I'm telling you now." He pulled her arm down and gazed at her, his face earnest. "Are you ready to risk the shock total ecstasy will bring to your system?"

Reaching up, she placed her hands on his shoulders and pushed him back on the bed. "I'm tough," she said, diving to kiss his nose and then his chin. "But if you doubt that I'll hold up, you could always give me a trial run right now."

He gazed at her sternly. "I'm sorry. I don't give out free samples of ecstasy."

"How stingy," she said in indignation. "I don't know whether I'll give you my business or not."

Her bare neck was too much for him to resist. He raised his head to nuzzle it, and said lazily, "I suppose I could manage a little rapture." He bit her shoulder. "Or bliss." His tongue laved her collarbone. "Or maybe even a little mad frenzy." Grasping her shoulders, he raised her slightly, holding her above him so that he could take one nipple into his mouth. When a low sound of pleasure broke from her, he rolled with her until he was on top, looking down at her. With a husky laugh he whispered, "But don't expect ecstasy."

A moan of frustration escaped her, and Helen moved her thighs to accommodate him. His teasing was driving her wild. Digging her fingers into his bare buttocks, she urged him closer. She had to have him now.

And although he told her not to expect it, the next half hour was an ecstasy that only morning love can be. The desperation of the night before was missing, but not the urgency. Their lovemaking celebrated a oneness of mind and body that came with new understanding.

When next she could think rationally, Helen found Tom staring down at her silently. She reached up to caress his strong face, his warm shoulder. "If that was only a sample," she whispered, her voice husky and breathless, "I'm definitely buying the product."

He laughed in delight and hugged her close. "Oh, love. I feel like I could stay here in bed with you for the rest of my life."

"And I can't think of a better way for you to spend your time," she said smartly. Then she moaned. "The time. I've got to go back to the house. There are a thousand and one things to do."

"As much as I hate to say it, I guess you're right," he said reluctantly. "I don't think you would enjoy being caught sneaking in the house in your nightgown at noon."

She glanced around the bed, then leaned down

to look at the floor beside the door. "Speaking of my gown, what happened to it?"

He looked down at his feet under the covers and wiggled his toes vigorously. "There's a very suspicious lump under my feet."

She laughed. "I knew it. One way or another I knew that I would end up wearing your footprints."

After being bunched up all night, the gown was badly creased, and Helen wished she had had the foresight to wear a robe the night before. Although it might seem odd to anyone who saw her, she decided to borrow a royal blue bathrobe from Tom. At least it covered her and kept her from feeling quite so exposed.

She strolled in an exaggeratedly casual manner across the terrace, then ducked quickly into the study. Stage one successfully completed, she thought, laughing breathlessly as she moved across the room and into the entry hall.

Helen almost made it. Her foot was on the bottom step of the stairway when the front door opened wide.

She whirled around in surprise, then grabbed the banister to keep her balance. She had expected to be confronted with curiosity, but the look on her daughter's face was far from curious.

Audrey was standing in the doorway with an overnight case in her hand. Audrey had always been fastidiously neat, but she didn't look neat now. She looked as though she had dressed in the dark. Her eyes were red-rimmed from crying, her face desperately unhappy.

"Audrey," Helen said in concern, moving toward her daughter. "What is it, darling?"

The younger woman's lips quivered. She tried to speak, but the sound died in her throat. Catching back a sob, she dropped the suitcase and ran to her mother.

Helen wrapped her arms around her daughter protectively, feeling her tremble. "What's happened? Are you all right? Where is Chad?"

"Chad!" her daughter said, spitting out the word. "I don't ever want to hear his name again."

"What's he done now?"

"He—" She broke off, shaking her head. "I can't even say it. I knew things weren't right between us. But I never imagined anything like this."

"Audrey, you're scaring me," Helen said. "Tell me what's happened."

"I found out last night that—that Chad is having an affair." She said the words in a rush and drew away to bury her face in her hands.

"Audrey," Helen whispered in shock. "He couldn't— Are you sure?"

Audrey nodded vigorously. "Yes. He never came home last night. And this morning he refused to tell me where he'd been." She raised tear-filled eyes. "I couldn't stay there with him. You can see that, can't you?"

Helen ran harried fingers through her hair. "Yes—yes of course. I understand."

"Mother," Audrey said hesitantly, biting her lip. "Can I come home?"

Helen's heart twisted in sympathy. "Oh, darling,

of course you can." She felt helpless. "I'm just so sorry it happened. Is there anything I can do?"

"No, I just want to go to bed." She smiled thinly. "I haven't had much sleep lately."

She turned to walk wearily up the stairs, and Helen stared after her. She was worried about her daughter's health, about the baby. The doctor had warned Audrey about stress. What was all this doing to her? Helen wondered.

At that moment Gary swung around the top of the stairs, stopping abruptly to stare at his sister as she passed him without speaking.

He glanced over his shoulder as he moved toward Helen. When he reached his mother at the bottom of the stairs, he asked quietly, "What's wrong?"

"Audrey has left Chad, Gary," Helen explained wearily. "She's moving back with us."

He stopped abruptly as her words sank in. He looked startled and concerned but beneath it all was a desperate kind of confusion. Helen knew exactly what he was feeling. Their lives were changing, and the changes were coming too fast.

Without a word he turned and started up the stairs after his sister. Helen caught his arm. "I think she needs to be alone right now, darling. You can talk to her later."

He turned back reluctantly then began to search his mother's face. Almost against his will, he reached out to hug her. "Don't worry so much," he said. "It'll all turn out right."

"I hope so," she said, trying to smile. "But I worry about the baby."

He frowned thoughtfully, and Helen took the

opportunity to inspect his face. Her son had apparently had a rough couple of days. He looked tired. There were dark circles under his eyes, eyes that were noticeably bloodshot.

"You don't look so hot," she said wryly. "What have you been doing to yourself?"

He shrugged. "I'm afraid I had a head-on collision with a beer keg."

He hesitated, staring down at the floor. "Mom," he said tentatively, his voice a little stiff. "I was out of line the other day. I'd . . . I'd like to apologize." He inhaled deeply, shoving his hands into the pockets of his jeans. "When I left for college, you accepted me as an adult. I guess I owe you the same courtesy."

Helen smiled. She knew how hard it was for Gary to admit he was wrong. "We'll forget it happened," she said.

"Thanks," he said, smiling in relief. "I know I acted like a nerd, but—"

"Go ahead," she prompted quietly. "I want to know how you feel."

He avoided her eyes as though the subject still made him very uncomfortable. "Just be careful with that guy," he muttered. "Will you do that?"

Without giving her a chance to respond, he moved toward the front door. "Now I think it's time I had a little talk with my brother-in-law."

"Gary—" Helen began urgently. But he had already disappeared.

His protective instincts were certainly being overworked on this trip home, Helen thought helplessly. She stood there for a moment, unable to decide what to do next.

"What a mess," she whispered to the empty hall. Then, running her fingers through her hair in frustration, she turned to go in search of Patty. Someone should tell the housekeeper what was going on.

Helen's thoughts were chaotic when she left the kitchen. She knew she should be calling people, making arrangements for her departure. Someone would have to take over the records for the Helping Heart center. And someone would have to take responsibility for the organization of the annual cancer drive.

But she couldn't seem to get in gear. The first thing she had to do was talk to her children. Everything else could wait. Although Helen had known all along that telling them would be difficult, she had been avoiding even the thought of it, as though that would make it go away.

"I'm such a coward," she muttered to herself as she went upstairs to dress.

In her bedroom she walked to the closet and looked inside. All those clothes, she thought, biting her lip. What should she take and what should she leave behind? Why had no one ever taught her the proper way to pack for life in a Winnebago?

"Why am I worrying about clothes?" she murmured aloud. But she knew this worry over trivia was simply a diversion. She was using it to keep her mind off the important things: Audrey; her grandchild; Gary; Tom.

No, Helen thought, she didn't have to worry

about Tom. He was the one sure thing, the one solid thing in her life now. But before she could begin the future, she had to be strong enough to clear up the past.

Shaking her head in frustration, she walked to the bathroom to shower. She glanced around, seeing everything as though for the first time—the crystal vase Edward had brought back from Italy for her, the giant flagon of perfume from Paris.

She closed her eyes and let her mind slide back to the past. It was time that she faced the truth and let go of the lie. Life with Edward had not been perfect, as she had always tried to pretend. After the first couple of years there had been no real communication between them.

Helen shivered slightly when she remembered the silent loneliness. The fact that she'd refused to admit it existed had only made it worse. The births of her children had helped her to hide it. She had turned to them for companionship and affection. For so many years she had been there when her children needed her. And although she hadn't admitted it consciously, they had always been there for her. The three of them shared a kind of closeness that was becoming rare in the modern family. That was one of the reasons she was filled with such confusion at the thought of leaving them.

The other reason was harder to define. If she had failed in her marriage with Edward, would she not also fail in her marriage to Tom? Would she disappoint him as she had disappointed Edward? Would he gradually grow away from her?

Although she desperately wanted to live up to his

expectations, Helen was very much afraid she was destined not to.

She raised her chin stubbornly and left her bedroom. It was time to talk to Gary and Audrey. Regardless of her doubts, Helen wasn't about to throw away what she had with Tom. She would simply face things as they came. She would *make* things right.

Tom was standing in the doorway of the Winnebago, looking out across the lawn toward the house. Helen had been gone for a long time. He needed to talk to her about where they would go next. They had the whole country to consider. He wanted her to have a say in their future. They would be a team from now on. The perfect team.

How was he ever going to be able to convey to her how much she had come to mean to him? Somehow it seemed risky to love someone as much as he loved Helen. It was almost like tempting the gods.

He shook the thought away. He couldn't allow negative emotions to get the better of him.

For a moment longer he stood looking at the house, then he stepped down and began walking toward it. Maybe it was silly, but a curious anxiety was building in him. He would go see what was taking her so long. If he could just touch her, everything would be all right.

Helen had to wait three hours to pin her children down at last. Gary walked into the house just minutes before Audrey came downstairs, looking pale and tired. Helen watched her daughter with concern as the three of them went into the study to talk quietly of inconsequential things.

After a while Helen began to probe delicately. It would certainly help if Audrey's problem with Chad could be resolved before she and Tom left town. But no matter how many times Helen asked her, Audrey stubbornly refused to discuss her husband.

Finally Helen couldn't put it off any longer. She had to tell them she was leaving with Tom. Although she tried to convince herself that they would be happy for her, she dreaded testing that theory.

She bit her lip and glanced at her children from beneath her lashes. They didn't look very receptive, she thought in resignation.

Straightening her back, she said, "Audrey. Gary." When they turned to look at her, she smiled. "I need to talk to you both."

Audrey stiffened in her chair, her young mouth held in belligerent lines. "I've told you, Mother. I won't talk about Chad."

"No, no," her mother soothed. "It's not about Chad this time."

"Well, if it's about that English lit grade," Gary said hastily, "I can explain."

Helen chuckled. "No, it's not your grades either." She paused, drawing in a deep breath. "I know my timing may be a little off, but it can't be helped."

"What's up?" Gary said, his eyes growing curious.

Helen cleared her throat. "You both know Tom and—"

Suddenly the two pairs of eyes that had been trained on her face were gazing over her shoulder. Helen turned in her chair. Tom was standing in the doorway.

Gary stared at Tom for a moment in silence, antagonism growing in his slender face. Then he turned back to look at Helen in astonishment. "What's he doing here?" he asked in outrage. "You were about to say something about—about *him* and you. What was it?"

"Mother?" Audrey said hesitantly. "Mother, what's going on?"

Helen stood up and moved to stand beside Tom, saying as she walked, "Calm down, both of you."

Tom's lips twisted in an apologetic smile as he gazed down at her. "I'm sorry," he said softly. "I take it you haven't told them yet."

She slid her hand in his. "Don't apologize."

"Told us what?" Gary demanded.

Helen turned back to face them, darting a smile of gratitude at Tom when she felt his arm slide around her waist. "I was trying to tell you before that Tom and I are going to be married."

"*No*," Gary rasped out harshly as he came awkwardly to his feet.

Audrey sat wide-eyed on the couch, looking as though someone had just knocked the air out of her. "Mother," she said, her voice faint and shocked. "Mother . . ." Whatever she had intended to say was forgotten, and she simply sat there staring at Helen and Tom.

"You're crazy," Gary said, moving closer, fists clenched in anger. "You can't do this."

Audrey slowly stood up, supporting her ungainly body on the arm of the chair. "Mother, I can't believe you mean that. An affair is one thing, but *marriage*. Would you let him live in Daddy's house?" Then with her voice lowered, she said, "But he's the gardener."

"Thank you for pointing that out, Audrey," Helen said dryly. "But I had already noticed."

She was aware of Tom shaking with laughter, and immediately Helen felt better. The situation couldn't be too bad if he could still find something amusing about it.

But apparently Gary didn't find it the least bit amusing. "He's after your money," he said bluntly, his eyes blazing as he stared at Tom. "I can't let you do this." He moved closer to Tom. "I think you'd better leave now."

"Gary!" Helen said. "Regardless of what Audrey said, this is *my* house. You don't have the right to order people out of it."

Audrey shook her head helplessly. "But he's the gardener," she repeated, her voice faint.

Helen smiled wryly. "I'm afraid I made a few mistakes in teaching you values, Audrey. No matter what you think, if a gardener is good enough to sleep with, he's good enough to marry."

"Mother!"

Helen continued as though her daughter hadn't spoken. "And this particular gardener is good enough for anything." She looked sadly from her daughter to her son, trying to remember that they had had a shock. "I never thought I would say this, but I'm ashamed of you both."

Tom glanced at her and said quietly, "Maybe it would be better if I left you alone."

She turned to face him and said under her breath, "If I had a choice, I would go with you and leave *them* alone." She sighed in resignation. "But I guess I'd better get it straightened out."

When Tom smiled at her, Helen forgot the other two in the room. "I trust you. You'll handle it just right," he said softly. "How long do you think we'll have to wait? Howie's coming back to work tomorrow. I'd like to call and make reservations for a space in a park I've heard about near Hot Springs."

"Arkansas?" she began when Audrey broke in from right behind Helen.

"What are you talking about?" the younger woman asked, her voice slightly hysterical. "Mother, you're not leaving? You didn't say anything about leaving!"

Helen turned to face her daughter. "That's enough, Audrey. Calm down."

"But you're leaving!" she whispered, her voice desperate. She was strangely flushed, and her breathing sounded harsh and rapid.

Helen looked from Audrey to Gary then back again. She had known it would be difficult, but she hadn't realized the deep pain she would feel on her children's behalf. Although Gary was trying very hard to look like a disapproving adult, there was a sheen of tears in his eyes. And Audrey obviously felt as though her mother were deserting her in her time of need. Helen had spent too many years feel-

MRS. GALLAGHER AND THE NE'ER-DO-WELL

ing every hurt either of them suffered to disassociate herself from them now.

She gazed at them both, her eyes pleading for their understanding. "If you had given me a chance earlier," she said, her voice slow and wary, "I would have told you both that when Tom leaves here, I'll be going with him."

Gary looked as though someone had struck him before he swung away, his fists clenched.

Suddenly Audrey swayed, and before Helen could react, Tom swept the pregnant woman up in his arms just as her eyes rolled to the back of her head.

"Take her to the couch," Helen said, moving with him. She arranged a cushion under her daughter's head. "Gary, get a wet cloth."

When Gary left the room, Tom asked, "What is it? What's wrong with her?"

"She's hyperventilated," Helen explained, her voice much steadier than her heartbeat. "She hasn't done this since she was in high school."

"And whose fault is it that it's happened this time?" Gary said from directly behind them, handing a damp washcloth to his mother. "You know the doctor said she should avoid stress. Now look at her."

"That's enough," Tom said quietly, his eyes trained on Gary.

The words weren't threatening. They were low and calm. There was even a kind of understanding in his expression. But only a fool would have refused to heed the warning. And although Gary was young and reckless, he wasn't a fool. He moved away to stare out the window.

Helen glanced down when her daughter whimpered and began to move her head. "Mother," Audrey said weakly.

"Everything's fine, darling," Helen said. "You just rest for a while."

When her mother stood, Audrey clutched at her hand. "Don't leave me," she said anxiously.

"I'll be right back."

Helen and Tom moved into the hall. The minute she closed the door behind them, Tom took Helen in his arms to hold her tightly. She sighed in relief. "You don't know how much I need this," she said, moving her face against his shoulder.

"I'm afraid I wasn't thinking of you," he said with a wry smile. "I just knew how much I needed it." He lifted her chin and stared into her eyes. "Do you know how proud I am of you? I had to bite my tongue a couple of times in there, but you stood tough."

She smiled. "I told you I was tough." Her smile faded as she reached up to stroke his face. "I'm sorry about all that. And I'm so desperately sorry that we won't be able to leave as soon as you wanted to."

His features froze and he backed away from her. "What are you talking about?"

She dropped her arms slowly to her side, staring at him in confusion. "But surely you realize I can't leave yet. Not with Audrey ill."

"You said she'd done this before," he answered tightly. "Is it serious?"

"No—no, not in itself," she admitted, hurt and bewilderment clouding her eyes. "But she's pregnant. This kind of tension is dangerous for her." When she stepped closer to him, he moved away, avoiding her eyes. "Tom," she said anxiously. "I know my children are a bit spoiled, but they're not bad. They love me. If we can just give it a little time, I know they'll both come to accept our marriage. And then I can leave without worrying."

A loud, harsh breath shuddered through his body. Then slowly he turned to face her.

"You say it's just for a little while," he said slowly. "And logically I can say, 'What's a few more weeks?' But in here"—he touched his chest with his clenched fist—"it feels as if I were being shoved aside. As if you had a choice to make and I'm not the one you chose."

He ran his fingers through his hair, frustration creating deep lines around his mouth. "One thing I'm sure of. If we wait until it's convenient, damn it, we'll never be together. If you let your children say what you should do now, it won't stop." He inhaled raggedly. "And I'll always remember that you didn't choose me."

Helen couldn't believe what she was hearing. She had never seen him like this. "You're being unreasonable," she said tightly. "You simply can't know what it's like to be a mother." She gestured toward the living room with a short wave of her hand. "Right or wrong, they depend on me. That isn't their fault. It's mine. And it's up to me to correct the situation." She stared up at him, her eyes pleading for understanding. "Can't you see? I owe them that much."

He was silent for a moment. When he spoke, the

words were sharp. "And how long do you think it will take?"

Helen had tried very hard to stay calm. But no one used that tone of voice with her. "It will take as long as it takes," she said, her voice shaking with anger.

He let out a slow breath and shook his head. "I won't do it," he said under his breath. "I *can't* do it." After taking a couple of agitated steps away from her, he turned and smiled grimly. "Audrey and Gary are just an excuse, aren't they? I should have known something like this would happen. You weren't exactly enthusiastic about leaving with me." He moved his shoulders as though they ached. "And if it weren't your children, it would be something else. From the beginning you've kept me out of your life."

He moved to the door. With his hand on the knob he said, "I think I've always known you didn't love me enough to make the break, to leave all this behind. I just didn't want to admit it." He opened the door. "You've made your choice. There's no need to drag it out."

And before she could defend herself, before she could tell him he was wrong, Tom walked out the door.

Ten

Almost a week later Helen sat in the living room, staring down at the magazine in her lap without seeing a word or a picture printed there. There was no vitality in her. She could have been another piece of furniture in the room for all the life she showed.

Helen had changed a lot in the past week; she looked now like a washed-out version of her former self. Her face was pale, and there were dark circles under her eyes. Her unhappiness was glaringly obvious.

Across the room Gary sat with his leg swung over the arm of an overstuffed chair. He had canceled his plans to visit friends in Florida. Helen had sensed him watching her all week, but she couldn't guess what was going on in his mind. And she didn't ask.

Audrey, looking much better than she had on that day a week before, was reclining on the couch.

She had not been in touch with Chad, and he had made no effort to call her. But even with her marital problems, Audrey had bloomed under Patty's indulgent care.

As Helen gazed listlessly about the room Audrey began to pick nervously at the pink nail polish adorning her long fingernails. Gary cleared his throat loudly and shifted in his seat. They both seemed uneasy, but Helen felt an odd kind of detachment as she turned her gaze away from her children to stare out the window.

"I can't stand it anymore!"

Helen turned in mild curiosity to find her daughter standing in the middle of the room. The younger woman's eyes were shining with tears as she began to pace the room. "I can't stand to see you so unhappy." She kicked at an ornamental straw basket on the floor. "No wonder Chad is sleeping around. Who could love such a selfish person?"

Helen gave a broken laugh. Her daughter had always leaned toward the dramatic. "Don't be so hard on yourself," she said quietly. "Pregnancy is a selfish time. It's all part of nature."

Gary stood up abruptly and walked to the window. "I wish I had such a good excuse," he said sadly. "But there is no excuse for the way I acted."

His back was stiff as he stood there. After a moment he turned back to face his mother, a strange, hesitant expression on his face. "I don't really know how to say this—I wish I didn't have to say it," he added, grimacing. "But it's been driving me crazy for a week, and I might as well get it over with. You're going to find out sooner or later."

"For heaven's sake, Gary," Audrey said in exasperation, her guilt losing itself in annoyance. She lowered her swollen body gingerly to the couch. "If you're going to say something, say it. You sound like you've done someone in and hidden the body in the basement."

"I wish that were all it was," he muttered. "The truth is, I've been offered a job that I can work at part-time through college. Then when I graduate, they'll start me out full-time in a good position."

"That's wonderful, Gary," Helen said softly. "Why didn't you want to tell us?"

He closed his eyes, his muscles tightening as though he were steeling himself for something. "Because the job is in Minnesota," he said at last. "I'll have to transfer and—and I won't be getting home very often."

"You—you *louse!*" Audrey said, jumping up again. "You're much worse than I am. You wanted Mother to stay home even though you wouldn't be here. Of all the insensitive—"

"Oh, can it, will you? You didn't act any better." He smiled grimly, his eyes gleaming. "It's me, remember. Your brother. The one who knows just exactly how you bring on those fainting spells."

Audrey darted a nervous look at Helen. When she saw no anger in her mother's eyes, she sank to the sofa and began to cry. "He's right," she said, sniffing loudly. "But I didn't really think about doing it. It just happened," she added helplessly. Then she raised her head, shooting her brother a furious glare. "That doesn't make what you did any better. At least I genuinely need Mother."

"Oh, yeah? Well, what about your husband? Why isn't he taking care of you?"

"You know why," she said, her voice trembling. "I refuse to live with a man who's sleeping with another woman."

"Bull," Gary said emphatically.

Audrey stared at him suspiciously. "Why do you say it like that?"

"It just so happens I talked to Chad," Gary said. "And he says you made the whole thing up. There is no other woman. He says you didn't even give him a chance to explain. But he's not going to beg you to come back because you're acting like a spoiled brat." He grinned. "I didn't know old Chad had it in him."

Audrey stood up awkwardly and moved to stand beside her brother. "Gary, do you mean it? Did he really say he wasn't having an affair?"

Her brother snorted contemptuously. "He would have told you himself if you hadn't accused him without waiting to hear the truth."

She twisted her hands anxiously. "I've got to go pack," she murmured. "I've got to go home." She looked up at Gary. "Will you drive me?"

"I guess so," he said as they walked together toward the door. "But don't take all day. I have to meet some friends in an hour."

"I promise I'll hurry," she said, her eyes shining with excitement. "Mother can help me—"

Suddenly they both stopped and turned back to

Helen. She hadn't moved during the entire conversation.

"Oh, Mother," Audrey said in sympathy. "What are you going to do?" She bit her lip. "Do you think you could tell Tom that you've changed your mind?"

Leaning her head back wearily, Helen said, "I don't know where he is. He said he was going to Hot Springs next." She smiled sadly, remembering how he had told her they would explore the world together. "I've called all the parks in the area, but he isn't at any of them."

She examined the surprised expressions on her children's faces. "Did you think I was waiting for your permission?" she asked drily. "I knew I had made a mistake thirty minutes after he left the house. But by then it was too late. The motor home was gone."

"I know where he is," Gary said quietly.

Helen's head came up sharply at the softly spoken words. She stood and moved to face her son. "What are you talking about?"

"He's still here at the state park."

"How do you know that?" she said, her voice urgent, her hands beginning to tremble.

Gary turned a brilliant red. "I'm not proud of what I did," he said defensively. "But at the time I thought it was for your own good."

"Gary."

He shoved his hands in his pockets, looking very much like a small boy caught in an act of mischief. "I paid someone to keep an eye on him," he muttered at last. "Rafe Hampson needed to make some extra money so he's been hanging around at the state park for me, asking questions and keeping an eye on Tom. When Tom checked in, he told the park ranger that he would be at the park for a week."

"Rafe Hampson?" Audrey said, rolling her eyes. "Really, Gary, he's the sleaziest man in town."

Gary looked uncomfortable, then slightly belligerent. "I didn't exactly have a large selection of spies to choose from. What did you want me to do—take out an ad?"

"But Rafe Hampson?" Audrey repeated.

He shrugged. "I had to do something. I was afraid Tom would come back here, and I wanted to know about it before Mom did."

Helen smiled, torn between affection and exasperation. "You know and I know that what you did was wrong, but somehow I can't be angry with you for doing it. Not if it means I'll have a chance to see Tom again." She frowned. "If he intended to stay only a week, that means he'll be leaving today."

Helen ran trembling fingers through her hair, trying to decide what to do next. But her brain couldn't get past one incredible thought—Tom had waited for her.

Audrey squeezed her mother's hand. "Are you going out there now?" she asked, smiling.

"No." Helen shook her head. "I've got to come up with a way to overcome this misunderstanding. He was too deeply hurt. I've got to convince him that I'm one hundred percent with him."

"But how will you do that?" Audrey asked.

Helen shrugged. "I don't know. I'll think of something." Her eyes were blazing with a secret fire. "I've got to."

It was much later in the day when Helen began to wonder if she had really found the right way to convince Tom. She winced as she glanced at her figure in the bedroom mirror. Then after a moment she began to smile. It wasn't that bad, she thought suddenly. In fact, Helen thought she might even get used to it . . . someday.

Turning away from the mirror, she began to place various articles of unfamiliar clothing into an old suitcase. The case was Patty's. It was an old one her housekeeper had been saving for the next charity sale.

When the clothes were neatly packed, Helen walked to the closet. Reaching up, she pulled a round box from the top shelf then walked back to lay it on the bed beside the case. Now she had everything.

She sank slowly to the bed, rubbing her brow to ease the tension within her. She was taking such a chance. Even after all her preparations, her plan might not work. But she had to try.

She had spent all morning working out the details. On Gary's instructions the man he had hired would keep in touch with Helen, letting her know when it was time to put her plan into action.

Once more she glanced at her image in the mirror. The difference in her appearance amazed her. If this didn't work, she would absolutely die of embarrassment, she thought, grinning crookedly.

Then the smile faded, and she closed her eyes in silent prayer. It had to work. It simply had to.

Tom stood looking around at the pine trees that had become his silent companions in the week just passed. He smiled slightly. The trees had heard a lot of strong language in that time.

Slowly he leaned down to pick up a metal pan he had used to feed the birds. It was the last bit of packing he had to do. Everything was ready.

Everything except his heart, he thought sadly.

Glancing around, he frowned. He felt as though he were forgetting something. He checked the camping space one more time but found nothing. Inhaling deeply, he knew that there was nothing more to hold him here. It was time to move on.

He took his time driving along the narrow, winding road, glancing to the right, then to the left. Although it was strange, he wished he could memorize every tree, every flowering bush. He didn't want this place to fade from memory.

When he passed through the front gate of the park, he noticed a man standing beside a car parked behind the combination store and Laundromat.

Strange, Tom thought. He had seen the same man several times during the week. He was always near the store. And he always acted guilty about something.

"He's probably cheating on his wife," Tom murmured, shrugging. Though if that was the problem, the man had certainly picked a strange place to carry on an affair.

Tom pulled the Winnebago into the gravel driveway and stopped before the gas pump. While the tank was being filled, he leaned against the motor home, his eyes examining the area as closely as he had the woods. He had been doing the same thing all day. He knew how much time he would spend thinking about this place in the future. He wanted the scenery indelibly imprinted in his mind. He didn't want to forget a single detail.

Beside him Tom heard gravel shifting underfoot and glanced toward it. The man he had seen earlier now leaned casually against the pump.

"These babies sure hold a lot of gas," the man said, his eyes darting from the Winnebago to the store and back again. His gaze slid past Tom, but never once did he look him in the eyes.

"Uh-huh," Tom murmured, in no mood for idle chitchat, especially with such a jumpy man. It made Tom nervous just to watch him.

When the gears on the pump continued to turn, the stranger said, "You must be getting ready to go quite a distance." He looked at Tom questioningly.

"Yeah, I guess," Tom said. Then he nodded shortly. "Yes, I guess I am."

"You travel a lot?"

Tom was a patient man. He was a kind man. But idle curiosity was the last thing he wanted to face right now. He shifted his stance and nodded. "Yes."

Even the most dense person would have recognized the bluntness of the answer. The stranger was only momentarily taken aback. He cleared his throat, gazed up at the sun and said, "That's something I've always wanted to do. Travel, you know."

Tom grunted in agreement, watching the pump, willing it to hurry up so he could leave. Luckily at that moment, the pump clicked off.

Before the man could continue the unwanted conversation, Tom replaced the gas nozzle. Nodding abruptly, he turned away. When he had paid for his purchase and said good-bye to the elderly woman who ran the store, Tom returned to the Winnebago.

The strange, fidgety man was nowhere in sight. But as Tom pulled away from the station he glanced in the rearview mirror. The man was standing in the driveway watching him. After a moment he turned and walked to the telephone booth.

Two seconds later the stranger was forgotten as Tom headed toward Langston for the last time.

Helen inhaled shakily. She held her head higher, firming her chin as people began to stare. She had expected to create a stir. In fact, it was part of the plan. She wouldn't let it bother her, she told herself. She would be strong—for Tom, for herself.

Suddenly a crooked smile curved her lips. She would be strong, she thought wryly, but she sure hoped Tom would come soon. According to Rafe Hampson, Tom had left the park fifteen minutes earlier. No matter which direction he intended to follow once he left town, he had to come through Langston first.

Tom slowed the Winnebago on the outskirts of Langston. He knew it wasn't fair of him, but he resented the town that lay before him. The town had won and he had lost. He wished he didn't have to go through it, but it was the only way to get to the Interstate.

He hadn't been in town for a week. The longest week of his life, he mused. A week was enough time for her to change her mind if she was going to. It was long enough for her to decide to come to him. He inhaled to steady himself.

He wanted her with a desperation that was foreign to him. But if she couldn't "forsake all others" now, in the heat of new love, what would it be like later?

Suddenly the traffic on the main street began to slow. Tom frowned. Somehow it seemed appropriate that the one time he was in a hurry, Langston would be hit by an unheard-of traffic jam. It was as though the town were taking its last opportunity to rub salt in Tom's wound.

Traffic moved forward a little. He could see a crowd gathered on the sidewalk ahead, but his thoughts were too taken up with Helen and his own unhappiness even to wonder what was going on.

He had wanted to find out about life, he mused, giving a short, harsh laugh. Well, he had found out. Life was inconsistency. A week ago he had been happier than ever before. He had never known it was such a short walk from heaven to hell.

Tom heard muffled laughter from the crowd on the sidewalk ahead, but didn't really take it in. A deep anxiety was growing inside him. Now that he was on the point of leaving, he was becoming obsessed with details.

He kept seeing Helen as she had looked on the day of the picnic. And the way she had studied him so closely after the first time they made love. The way she always laughed, as though she were a little surprised by her own laughter. Helen, silver-tinted in moonlight, warm and golden in the sun.

Why? he thought, tapping his thigh with one clenched fist. Why hadn't she loved him enough to change? Why hadn't she cared enough to see it his way?

Suddenly a strange expression twisted his features, an expression of disbelief. And after a moment he closed his eyes slowly in pain.

He simply couldn't believe his own thoughts. Why hadn't he listened to himself before? He was expecting her to do all the changing, to give up everything! The colossal nerve of the notion absolutely floored him. Who did he think he was anyway? he wondered in self-disgust.

He had spent so much time on anger and self-pity, he hadn't even stopped to consider the fact that he was asking Helen to make all the sacrifices. She could have turned the whole thing around and demanded that he stay as a test of his love.

But she hadn't. She had agreed to give up her

entire way of life if that was what he wanted. She had simply needed time to get her children used to the idea.

He inhaled a harsh breath. It was time he came to grips with his antagonistic feelings toward Gary and Audrey. Maybe they were used to a little too much of their mother's time, but basically they were good, decent people.

The truth was Tom was jealous. He winced as he admitted it to himself at last. If it had been anyone else, he would have tried harder to understand; he would have been more considerate. But it wasn't anyone else. It was Helen, and, right or wrong, he was as possessive as hell.

The deeper Tom delved into his heart and mind, the greater his dismay became. All the blame rested on his own shoulders. From the beginning he had taken pride in the fact that he had taught her to open up to life, but he had conveniently overlooked what Helen had taught him. She had taught him that freedom wasn't running away. Freedom was loving and giving and sharing.

He had become so obsessed with his quest that he hadn't stopped to think that the truth of life was everywhere. With Helen beside him he knew he could carry that truth into even the fast-paced business world. Because it didn't matter what a man did or where he was or what was going on around him. What mattered was inside.

Suddenly he knew he had to go to her. Nothing was worth a damn if he didn't have Helen. He would do it her way. If she wanted to stay, then they would stay. He would do anything, be anything, to keep her.

He leaned his head out of the window to see if the cars ahead were moving, but could see nothing. The traffic jam had probably been caused by a fender bender, he thought in exasperation. That was such a rare occurrence in Langston that no doubt everyone had stopped to offer advice.

Opening the door, he stepped out. He would see for himself what was holding up traffic. And if the problem wasn't cleared up soon, then Tom would simply walk to her house. One way or the other he had to see Helen right away.

He started walking toward the crowd on the sidewalk, his thoughts torn between what was happening now and what would happen as soon as he had her in his arms again. When he drew closer, it occurred to him that it couldn't be an accident or the crowd would have gathered in the street. He frowned. It wasn't noisy enough to be a fight.

As he reached the group the people who saw him began to fall silent, giving him what he could only call peculiar looks. He could see the top of a sign at the center of the crowd and wondered in frustration if he had stumbled onto some kind of demonstration. He moved closer, and silently the crowd began to part for him.

When Tom had almost reached the center, his steps slowed, then he stopped in his tracks, closing his eyes briefly as his heart began to pound in his chest.

Helen was sitting on a suitcase in the middle of the sidewalk. He felt his mouth go dry in reaction when he saw the tight, worn jeans clinging to her long legs. A black T-shirt was hugging her breasts, and her beautiful hair was falling about her shoulders.

After a stunned moment when his emotions seemed to explode chaotically, Tom laughed. It was a hearty, uninhibited sound, a sound of pure joy. The sign he had caught a glimpse of earlier was resting awkwardly on her shoulder. Printed on it in bright pink letters were the words ECSTASY OR BUST.

When Helen heard his laughter, she swiveled on the suitcase, then slowly, hesitantly, she stood up. Her nerves felt as if they were being stretched to the breaking point. She couldn't do anything other than stare silently.

Tom felt his heart jerk. He searched her face and knew as surely as if she had told him that she hated the avid attention she was attracting. She hated it, but she had done it anyway. For him. For the love of him.

He stared for a moment into her blue eyes. Beneath the embarrassment her eyes were wary, as though she were afraid of pain.

Stepping forward, he gently removed the sign from her grasp and, without taking his eyes from her, handed it to a short, stocky man who stared at it in confusion.

"It's time to go," Tom said gently.

Tears were shining in her eyes as she nodded her head vigorously. Tom stooped to pick up the suitcase, then turned to wrap his arm around her waist in a protective gesture.

"Wait," she said suddenly. Her voice was breathless as she pulled away from him momentarily to lean down and pick up a round box.

"It's a little pretentious for a motor home," she said, holding the box against her breasts. "But I happen to have a sentimental attachment to this hat."

Tom smiled slowly, remembering the beautiful blue hat. Remembering the day he had fallen in love with her eyes. He pulled her closer, and together they walked toward the Winnebago, toward the beginning of the rest of their lives.

Eleven

Helen held a bowl of salad in one hand and the ketchup in the other as she pushed the screen door open with her hip. Letting it slam behind her, she stood for a moment and looked out over the river. Then unerringly her eyes sought her family.

Tom was neglecting the steaks on the grill to give their squealing granddaughter a piggy-back ride. Amanda was two years old now and the pride of Audrey and Chad, who stood on the sidelines laughing. Gary and his most recent girlfriend were sitting under a pecan tree, their heads together as they talked earnestly.

Helen smiled. She believed Gary had finally met his match in Karen and the thought pleased her.

Placing the food on the picnic table, Helen found her thoughts going back to the beginning, to all the doubts and misunderstanding that had marked the early days of her relationship with her husband.

At the time their problems had seemed so very serious. Then with their honeymoon—that incredibly beautiful honeymoon—all the problems had dissolved like bad dreams in the morning sun.

They had spent two months on the road, going wherever their fancies took them, enjoying ecstasy in regular doses. Then they had returned to Langston for the birth of their darling Amanda. Tom had been intrigued by the perfect little human being from the very beginning. It had been at his insistence that they'd bought the chalet on the river, so they could return for regular visits.

Helen had wanted to sell the house that Edward had given her, but eventually Tom convinced her that it should belong to Audrey and Gary.

She closed her eyes when she felt warm lips on the back of her neck, strong arms around her waist.

"Is this what I married you for?" Tom said against her skin. "To stand around and daydream? Why did you let the steaks burn?"

She turned in his arms. "I believe the steaks were your department." She inhaled the earthy smell of spring. "I love it here," she murmured. "Are you sure you can't take another couple of weeks off?"

His dark eyes were serious as he stared down at her. "Do you really want to? I could probably work something out."

She shook her head, laughing in joy, because she had Tom, who loved her so very much, and because it felt good to be alive. "You may be able to get more time off, but I can't."

A few minutes later she watched him turn the steaks—they were only a little burned—and thought about how strange life was. When they had met, Tom was trying to get away from the hectic demands of the business world. And Helen had felt that her multiple roles in Langston society were deadening her soul. Now, two years later, they were living in Upstate New York, both engaged in occupations very similar to those they had run away from. Yet they were enjoying life immensely.

They had gone back to his home state so that Tom could convince himself that the discoveries he'd made in his travels held true in the rat race, too. He needed to prove that he could remain sane and whole in that world.

And they had gone back for Helen so that she could stretch and grow. So that she could test her ability to confront a larger portion of the world. She needed to see if she could expand the organizational skills she had gained in Langston to meet broader requirements.

And it had worked for both of them. The satisfaction of having successful careers only added to the fulfillment they found in each other. In the past two years they had grown as close to each other as two people can.

"Helen," Tom called. "Come see what Amanda's doing now."

"Yes, Mom. Come see."

Helen raised her eyes to the blue skies and whispered, as she did at least once a day, "Thank you." Then she walked to join her family.

THE EDITOR'S CORNER

As I write this Editor's Corner, it is the end of September 1985. (Books have to go into Production nine months before publication, as I told you a few months ago, but I'm given a little extra time to keep my comments as up to date as possible.)

The questionnaires from our October 1985 books are pouring in to the office. We rushed to do a preliminary analysis on the first few hundred to arrive because we were *very* curious! And, so far, we are delighted because 50 percent of those of you who responded said the quality of our line has improved, 34 percent said it has remained the same, and only 16 percent believe the quality has declined. High marks from you for which all LOVESWEPT authors and staff are most grateful . . . and most mindful of the responsibility we have to you because of your trust in us.

Many, many of you included notes and letters. They were wonderful—even most of the critical ones because they were so constructive. For example, one lady wrote: "I have only been disappointed with one or two LOVESWEPTS over the years. I must say, though, that the books in the first year seemed a little better than those now, perhaps because they *were* so different from everything else on the market. Now we're used to them and *expect* to be surprised each month . . ."

One of the things we try very hard to avoid is novelty just for novelty's sake. We want—first and foremost—to publish *strong love stories*. But, of course, we want to continue our tradition of freshness and creativity. We encourage our authors to write from their imaginations and hearts, unrestricted by guidelines and tipsheets. We aren't timid here at Bantam . . . if we were, I suppose the LOVESWEPT line would never have been created.

And now to give you some glimpses of our next four offerings—none of which, I assure you, is timid!

(continued)

Can you imagine yourself as a beleaguered working woman whose apartment is a mess and whose home life is disorganized? (Unfortunately, I don't have to use one iota of imagination to conjure this situation, but I only hope you do!) If you can dream up this scene, you are ready to step into the high heels of Dusty Ross, heroine of **THE BUTLER AND HIS LADY,** LOVESWEPT #131, by Anne and Ed Kolaczyk. Let's go on imagining with the Kolaczyks . . . the household employment agency sends you a "prime candidate." Voila. Pat Mahoney, butler extraordinaire! Pat is brawny and gorgeous and a great cook and can he ever organize one's life and run a home with all the dynamism of a tycoon! Now, wouldn't you try to be a perfect lady when confronted by a consummate hunk of a man waiting on you hand and foot? Dusty certainly does try to behave herself. And Pat's behavior is above reproach . . . well, almost. We think you'll revel in the trials of this lovable pair as they try for domestic bliss under most unusual circumstances!

THE GRASS IS ALWAYS GREENER . . . is a charming tour de force pitting lovely Cara Bedford and her family against the next door neighbor Hank Sandusky. The Bedfords are ardent gardeners, and determined to win the town's beautiful garden contest. Hank's property is an eyesore (to put it mildly). Green thumb/black thumb aren't the only traits that keep the straightlaced lady and the irrepressible gent at odds. Hank's endearing attempts to spruce up his place for Cara result in an episode with spray paint that we hope you find as hilarious and really touching as those of us on the staff did!

Remember Jerome Mailer? Sami's "find," the young man from the streets she had installed in her warehouse and was putting through law school? Now Fayrene Preston has given Jerome his own love story in **MYSTERIOUS,** LOVESWEPT #133. In this intriguing tale that also will fully update you on the lives of Morgan, Jason, Sami and Daniel, we encounter Jerome as a mature and most successful lawyer. Some-

(continued)

what world-weary, Jerome meets a woman—"Jennifer, just Jennifer," she murmurs—and his life becomes dangerous . . . breathtakingly exciting . . . heartstoppingly emotional. He is pulled into the web of terror ensnaring Jennifer, while falling head over heels in love with this enigmatic beauty. This is one of Fayrene's most originally written, dramatic romances ever!

What does a romantic woman do when a dream of a man—who looks for all the world like a Viking prince of old—bolts into her life? You'll get the answer to that question in Marion Smith Collins's marvelous love story **OUT OF THE CLEAR BLUE,** LOVESWEPT #134. Heroine Molly finds Rand Eriksson utterly beguiling . . . and completely threatening to her emotions as he campaigns to win her, body and soul. But as he captivates her heart, he also reveals some alarming insecurities Molly has harbored all through her life. In a shatteringly emotional confrontation, Molly must grow quickly in wisdom and security . . . or lose the great love of her life, Rand. You won't want to miss this witty, yet quite intense love story.

Again, we thank all of you who gave us your resounding votes of confidence. And, we also thank those of you who took the time to give us constructive criticism. We read every one of your letters carefully and—even though the numbers are too great for me to respond to each of you personally—please know that this bleary-eyed editorial staff cares very much about what you have to say.

Warm wishes,

Sincerely,

Carolyn Nichols

Carolyn Nichols
  Editor
LOVESWEPT
Bantam Books, Inc.
666 Fifth Avenue
New York, NY 10103